Scrappy

Scrappy

Osmond
Molarsky

DODD, MEAD
& Company
NEW YORK

1   2   3   4   5   6   7   8   9   10

Library of Congress Cataloging in Publication Data

Molarsky, Osmond.
   Scrappy.

   Summary: After her talents are grudgingly recognized
and she is accepted as the only girl member of Joe's
Garage soccer team, eleven-year-old Scrappy feels let
down when the sponsorship changes and the feminine
owner of a dress shop becomes the new coach.
   [1. Soccer—Fiction]   I. Title.
PZ7.M7317Sc   1983   [Fic]   82-45991
ISBN 0-396-08120-7

To the village of Ross, California, 94957, where stuff like this happens all the time

1

Scrappy Bassett sat on the players' bench, tightening her laces and listening to the guys argue.

"I'm not playing on any soccer team with any girl," Hughie Digby announced.

"She's really good, Hughie. She really is."

"We saw her booting it around with some kids in a pickup game. You ought to see her shoot."

"Man, is she fast! She can really run."

"She's cute, too." Paul Finley was always noticing how cute some girl was.

"We could use her on the forward line. How about it, Coach?"

"Maybe we could get out of crummy next-to-last place in this crummy league, if she was with us."

More than anything in the world, Scrappy Bassett wanted to play on a boys' team. Growing up with two very large, very rough brothers had made girls' soccer seem to her like a slumber party. Not only that—the girls played only a few weeks in the fall, while the boys played most of the year. And

Joe's Garage was the team she naturally wanted to play on, even it was practically trailing in the league. Most of the players were in her room at school, and their home field, at Bagley Common, was only four minutes from her house, by bike, if she pedaled hard.

"That's my last word," Hughie insisted. "I'm not playing on any girls' soccer team."

Soccer had gotten so big in the county that it was like Little League, with local businessmen taking over as sponsors and coaches. Hughie Digby played center forward for Joe's Garage and was their high scorer. Without Hughie, it wouldn't be much of a team. It wasn't much of a team anyway, seldom climbing out of eighth place in a nine-team league. That afternoon, they had the west end of the field for practice. Quality Cleaners had the east end.

"Stop arguing and get back to practice, you guys," Joe urged them. Joe Palmer was a pretty good coach but not the greatest, and he did not have too much control over his gang. He was kind of old and didn't really know too much about soccer. The argument over Scrappy was continuing, and he tried again. "Hey, guys, I'll tell you what. Suppose we give this kid a tryout. Is that fair, Hughie?

Hughie did not answer, just took a shot on goal that hit the top bar. He had kicked from way too far behind the ball. Some of the team heckled him and said he was afraid of the competition. Maybe Scrappy would get his job at center forward, if they let her play.

Just then, Bruce Reilly had an idea. "How about you and her in a shoot-out, Hughie?" The idea was for each of them to take ten penalty shots, from twelve yards out, with the other defending the goal. If Scrappy scored more goals than Hughie, she played. If she didn't score more goals than Hughie, she didn't play.

"That's fair, Hughie. You got to admit it, Hughie!" Doug Preston insisted.

"I bet she takes you, Hughie."

"She's a sharpshooter, Hughie."

"Hey, Hughie—you chicken?"

Every guy on the team got in a crack at the center forward.

"Do it, Hughie!" said Doug. "You got to do it— for your honor."

Hughie just muttered something, nodded his head and took his place in the penalty area. Everyone cheered.

"Okay, Scrappy!"

"Come on, Scrappy!"

"Here's your chance!" Everyone was for her, excepting Hughie.

Scrappy got up from the bench and started toward the net. She was small for her age and looked younger than her eleven years, but she walked like a little Marine on dress parade, very straight and sure of herself. She looked determined. Taking her place in the goalie position, halfway between the posts, she said, "I'm ready."

"I'm keeping score," said the coach. So was everyone else. This was important.

The shoot-out that followed was close. Defending goal first, Scrappy stopped five of Hughie's best shots, let five get past her. The score, Hughie five goals. Now it was Scrappy's turn, and she drilled five swift ones past him into the net—he had stopped four. The score, five-five, with one shot left for Scrappy. Nothing had been said about a tie. To get on the team, she had to win the shoot-out. This one would tell the story.

Scrappy set up the ball, backed up to make her run at it, stood there for a moment and took a deep breath. A kid coughed. No one else breathed. Somewhere on the field a dog barked. Scrappy charged at the ball, and Hughie braced himself for a hard kick. Five feet from the ball, Scrappy put on the brakes and came to a dead halt, then walked up to the ball and gave it a sharp little tap with the inside of her right foot, skidding it along the ground toward the left-hand post. Hughie, who was set for a hard, high one off the instep, dove for the ball and ended up on his face, in the dust, as it swished into the netting behind him. Scrappy had won the shoot-out, six to five. The guys cheered and mauled her a little, the way they do when a guy makes a goal. She was one of the team now, and everyone seemed happy. All but Hughie, who just looked a little bit foolish.

"Shake hands with your new teammate, Hughie," the coach said.

Scrappy hesitated, then put out her hand and Hughie took it. Both felt silly. After all, they were in the same room in school.

2

Scrappy sat cross-legged on her bed, holding a mirror and making hideous faces at herself. If she did this for five minutes a day, night and morning, just maybe she could save herself from the awful thing her father had said, not long ago, would happen to her.

Way back when Laura Jean Bassett was five years old, her father had declared, "That kid is dynamite." He was talking about the way she stood up for herself with her two big brothers and with other older children on the block. She was not taking any little-kid treatment from anyone. "She's really scrappy," her father said, a little proudly. And that is what he began to call her—Scrappy. So did everyone else, and it wasn't long before very few people knew her real name. Then, when she was almost eleven, she overheard her father say, "Scrappy is getting to be a little beauty, just like her mother."

"Definitely no way!" thought Scrappy. She loved the way her mother looked, but if she had to go around being pretty all the time she was a girl, just to look like her mother when she grew up, forget it. Floramae Williams was the prettiest girl in the class, and she was so stuck up that she could hardly take a deep breath. She couldn't do anything else, either. She couldn't throw a baseball or a rock more than about five feet. She couldn't boot a soccer ball down a steep hill. She wouldn't even try to skin the cat on the playground rings. That was because she thought her underpants would show, which of course they would, because she always wore dresses. All Floramae could do was stand around and look cute or walk in a straight line with small steps and breathe carefully. Not only that, but boys acted weird and silly around her. That was a drag.

"If only you'd let me do something with your hair," Scrappy's mother would say. "You'd look so pretty."

"No way," Scrappy objected. "I like it the way it is." The way she had it was close to her ears, in a very short pony tail held with a rubber band.

"You look like a seal coming up for a fish, at Marine World," her cousin Rick had said one time.

That was all right with Scrappy. "I like seals," she said. She also liked Rick, who was three years older than she was but was always nice to her at family gatherings.

Scrappy's hair was naturally curly, when she let it out. That bothered her, too. What if people thought she curled it herself, like Floramae Williams? Worst of all, deep down in Scrappy's mind, was the fear that if she looked the way Floramae Williams looked, if she got the reputation for being pretty, maybe even the prettiest girl in the class, she might get stuck up and turn into a weirdo and act like Floramae or even worse. It might make boys act silly and dumb around her, treat her the way they treated Floramae and her best friend, Elaine Sorenson—like girls. Who wanted to be treated like a girl? Not Scrappy. It wasn't that Scrappy wanted to *be* a boy. She just wanted to be treated like one. Right now, she was doing quite well. She had gotten a regular starting position with Garage—left halfback—and she hoped things would stay that way. She had played in six games already, had scored one goal and had set up eight other scores for Hughie and for Ken Turner and had gotten credit for assists on every one of them. The team had moved up in the standings from eighth to sixth, and Scrappy didn't mind accepting some of the credit. Even Hughie Digby had said, "Way to go, Scrappy," at the end of the game with Car Wash.

"Scrappy!" It was her mother's voice, startling her out of her daydreams. "What in the world are you doing?"

"Making faces," said Scrappy.

"I can see that," said her mother. "I thought you didn't want to be pretty."

"I don't."

"Well, for your information, young lady, one way the great beauties of this world keep their good looks is by doing exactly what you are doing now— stretching their faces into unimaginably hideous shapes. It does wonders to firm up the skin and the muscles and preserve their beauty."

Scrappy, stunned by this news, stared blankly at her mother for five seconds, allowed her face to go back to its normal shape, dropped her mirror, looked up at the ceiling and toppled over backward on her bed. How could she win?

3

In northern California, the boys played soccer ten months out of the year, calling off a few games in winter on account of rain, and breaking only in July and August, when it was too hot to run full speed for sixty minutes. Baseball of course did not have that problem. The longest anyone ever ran, in baseball, was about thirty seconds, if they hit a homer. Scrappy had joined Garage early in October. By mid-November, the club had climbed to sixth place in the league, and there it stayed. It was discouraging, but at least Scrappy was sure of a place in the starting lineup of a boys' soccer team, and that was what mattered.

Then, not long before Christmas, something happened that changed the whole picture. One day, at practice, Joe simply announced, "Team, I'm selling the garage. I won't be your sponsor anymore."

"When?"

"I sold it already."

"No way. I don't believe it."

"Don't kid us, Joe."

No one wanted to believe it. Everyone was shocked.

"What are you going to do, Joe? Are you going away?"

"I'm retiring from business. I'm going to Hawaii, get a little sun, do some fishing. I guess it's time." Joe was old.

"So who's going to be our sponsor? The new owner?"

"Who you selling the garage to, Joe?"

"That's the problem," Joe said. "The new owner is tearing down the garage. He's buying the property next door, too, and he's going to build a row of little shops and a restaurant."

"There won't be any garage anymore?"

"That's right. Maybe, if you're lucky, another sponsor will pick up the team."

Who'd want to sponsor a sixth-place soccer club in a nine-club league? Nobody said it, but that's what everyone was thinking, including Scrappy. A winning team was good advertising. It was good for business. Who needed a sixth-place team?

"When are you leaving?" Gil Mathews asked.

"Not till I sell my house. That may take some time."

"Will you coach us till then?"

17

"You can count on that," Joe said.

"Maybe he'll never sell his house." That was wishful thinking on Scrappy's part. "Maybe he'll even decide not to move to the Islands." She did not half-believe that. She knew perfectly well that Joe's Garage no longer could be their sponsor and that old Joe Palmer was through coaching. She knew also that just about anything could come up now, in the way of a sponsor—or maybe nothing at all. That would mean the team was doomed, finished. Scrappy was worried. She might never get on another boys' team.

The goalie rolled a ball out toward her. She took two steps, hooked the ball with her instep and drilled it into the upper left-hand corner of the goal. It was a perfect shot.

4

"Scrappy, you're going to have to give up your room tonight and tomorrow night," Mrs. Bassett informed her daughter.

"Is Mike bringing Pam home again?"

"Yes, he is. He telephoned, this morning."

Scrappy's oldest brother was a senior in college at Santa Barbara, and Pam was his girl friend. Twice before, he had brought her home for a weekend, and Scrappy had slept on a cot set up in her parents' bedroom.

"Why can't I set the cot up in my room and sleep with Pam?"

"It's better this way, dear," her mother assured her.

Scrappy knew it would do no good to argue. She also felt that there was some mysterious grown-up reason for Pam having the room to herself, so she let the matter drop. Just the thought of having Pam there in the same house with her gave her a happy feeling. Pam was nice and treated her like a grown-up, never asking dumb questions about school and did she like her teacher and stuff like that. Scrappy also thought Pam was very pretty. Oh, not soft-pretty. No Sleeping Beauty, like certain people she knew were practicing to be when they grew up. Pam was very relaxed and laughed all the time at things Scrappy said when she was feeling frisky and good. Pam was the kind of girl friend she thought it was perfectly all right for her brother to have, and he could bring her home as often as he liked, so far as Scrappy was concerned.

Mike drove in with Pam just in time for dinner. Scrappy carried in Pam's overnight bag and showed her to her room.

"Thanks, Scrappy," Pam said. "I'm afraid I'm putting you out of your room again."

"That's okay," Scrappy assured her. "I hope the bed's all right."

"It will be, I'm sure."

At dinner, Scrappy thought Mike looked very old. His beard had grown quite thick, but it wasn't that. He just looked more serious and more like a man and acted as if he rather owned Pam. Right now, Mike was Scrappy's favorite brother, because she did not see him very often. Of course, she loved Josh, but he was a senior in high school and was always there for her to argue and fight with. Lately, though, he had taken to acting too grown-up and superior to argue with her. How can you win an argument when someone won't argue?

During dinner, Scrappy had to listen quietly to a lot of stuff about microbiology and electron microscopes and graduate schools and teaching fellowships. Pam had quite a lot of things to say, and Scrappy got the idea that she wanted to be a doctor someday. She couldn't figure out exactly what it was Mike wanted to be. Being a doctor seemed better than being a nurse, Scrappy thought. Floramae Williams was going to be a nurse. Scrappy never thought about what she was going to be. Just being herself, right now, was all she could handle.

During the night, Scrappy had to get up to go to the bathroom. Sleepy and confused, not in her own room, she wandered toward the light that was still on in the living room. Mike and Pam were sitting on the sofa doing arithmetic in a notebook. Scrappy was not against mushy stuff for grown-ups who liked it. When her mother and father were mushy together, sometimes, it made her feel happy. So now arithmetic seemed a funny thing for Mike and his girl to be doing on the living room sofa, late at night. She might have said so, if she had not been so sleepy.

"Scrappy, what are you doing up?" Mike asked her.

"Going in there," Scrappy explained. "What are you doing up? What time is it, anyway?"

"One thirty-five," her brother informed her.

Pam said, "We're trying to figure out how we can make ends meet."

"If you don't need my room, I think I'll go back in there and go to sleep," said Scrappy.

"Do what you have to do, then back to your cot in Mom and Dad's room!" Mike ordered her, aiming her toward the bathroom.

It wasn't until two or three days later, when Scrappy was wide awake and fully alert, that the whole scene returned to her, even including just what Pam had said. "What did Pam mean by that?" Scrappy asked her mother.

"Making ends meet?"

"Yes." Ends of what, Scrappy wondered.

"It's what we do here at the end of every month," her mother said. "If we're careful." Scrappy looked baffled, and her mother explained. "It's just an expression, dear. It means having enough money to pay all your bills."

"Oh," said Scrappy. She shrugged and made her Bugs Bunny face, prominently displaying her two upper incisors. What did making ends meet have to do with Mike and Pam? She would find out soon enough.

22

5

Eight men and a woman sat around the long conference table in the Pelican Room of the Town & Country Motel, out on Route 101. They did not know it, but they were getting ready to cast a dark cloud over Scrappy Bassett's soccer career. Scrappy, of course, knew nothing about it, either. Players seldom knew what went on behind the scenes at Youth Soccer Council meetings. Fred Rumstead, president of Rumstead Motors and sponsor of the team known as Motors, was speaking. He was chairman of the Council, and this was a special meeting of the Council's executive board. "Gentlemen, I'd like to introduce a guest this evening—Miss Mary Louise Bradford. That's John Taggart on your left, Miss Bradford. Bill Johnson. Abe Smith . . ." He went around the table, ending with Chester Clemson, who was sitting at Miss Bradford's right, looking very important, as if his shirt were stuffed with chicken feathers. Chester was owner of Clemson's Footwear, on Main Street, and sponsored a team that was usually up near the top of the standings in the league, if not first. CLEMSON'S FOOTWEAR was printed very large on the backs of their jerseys. It was one of the ways Chester kept the public reminded that he was in business.

Each member, in his turn, mumbled, "Glad to know you," or "How'd yuh do," in deep, macho voices.

Very sweetly, Miss Bradford said, "Pleased to meet you, John. Hello, Bill . . ." and so on around the table.

"Glad to have you with us this evening," Fred Rumstead continued. "Gentlemen, Miss Bradford is here on a very special mission, if I may say so. An unusual one, I might add. First, though, for those of you who do not already know it, Joe Palmer has finally sold his home and in one week will be shoving off for the Islands, lucky bum."

Everyone agreed that Joe was a lucky bum.

"That of course leaves his old team without a sponsor or a coach. Gentlemen, as I think some of you know, Miss Bradford has rented one of the new shops on Bagley Common. She plans to offer quality clothing and other items for the younger set. Am I correct?"

"Yes, you are."

"It's to be called The Mary Louise Shop. And can

we call you Mary Louise, Miss Bradford?"

"I would be honored," she said.

"Mary Louise hopes to be in business here for a long time, and I'm sure all of us here wish her all success. With this in mind she would like to take over the sponsorship of Joe's Garage—changing the name, of course, as is only fitting."

"Who would coach her team?" asked Abe Smith.

"I would coach," Mary Louise said. Her voice was soft and silky.

Several of the men gave little, uncomfortable coughs.

"Don't be fooled by a pretty face, gentlemen," Fred Rumstead said. "Mary Louise starred on the University's women's basketball team, and she captained the soccer team for two years. I gather she knows fundamentals as well as most of us and maybe better than some and can teach them to the boys. Mary Louise was also a teacher for several years, before she went into business."

"What did you teach?" John Taggart wanted to know. John's son played goalie for Shoe Store, as Clemson's Footwear was generally known.

"Science," she said.

"Could you get away for practices?"

"I'd plan on two days a week. I'd plan to take off at five and leave the store in charge of my assistant.

The team practices just across the street, so it would be most convenient."

"Have you any transportation for away games?"

"The van I use in my business. It holds eight safely. I understand there's always a parent or two with a station wagon, to help out. I'd also be very happy to provide new uniforms and equipment, including cleats, if you plan to allow them." Only sneakers had been allowed until now, to keep everything even.

"We're taking that up at our next meeting," the chairman said. Cleated soccer shoes were an expense not every sponsor could afford. "Well, gentlemen, what do you think? Are we ready for a lady coach in our soccer league?"

"No offense, Miss Bradford, but I don't think the team would go for it," Chester Clemson said. "Not a lady coach."

"Oh, sure they would," Ray Mason said. "What you mean is—you wouldn't go for it, Chester."

Everyone knew that Chester Clemson had a store that might lose a little business to The Mary Louise Shop, especially if she had the name of her store on the backs of the jerseys and the team won some games. That was good advertising. Her shop was going to sell children's shoes, as well as clothing. Mr. Clemson knew that. Not only that, everyone knew that he was even against girls playing on Little League baseball teams and had fought hard to keep them off, just two years ago.

"Get with it, Chester," urged Abe Smith.

"This is the nineteen-eighties," Al Thompson reminded him.

"The team already has a girl on it, by the way," said Charlie Sanchez. "Did you know that?" He was needling Chester.

"Yes, I know that," said Chester, looking needled.

"And a very good player, too. Jerry Bassett's kid. They call her Scrappy."

"I move we put it to a vote of the whole council at Tuesday night's meeting," Horace Monkton said. The entire Council consisted of eighteen men, sponsors and other supporters of youth soccer in the county.

"Second!" a couple of voices said at once.

The motion passed to put the question to a vote of the entire Council on Tuesday.

"I think you can count on getting the team, Mary Louise," the chairman assured her, as the meeting broke up. "It's a low-ranking team, but that's your problem," he added.

"Thank you all," said Mary Louise. "You've been very nice. It would be an honor to be a part of your association—and to coach the team." Softly, to the chairman, she said, "I'll keep my fingers crossed."

She merely smiled nicely at Chester B. Clemson.

6

Wednesday, after school, Scrappy went to the city with her mother and brother Josh, to visit their grandmother. It was a good half-hour's drive from Bagley, over the Golden Gate Bridge, so she missed practice. It probably was just as well. That day, Joe said good-bye to the team—he was leaving next morning. The team gave him a "Two, four, six, eight . . ." He had been a pretty good coach, always there for practice, and they appreciated him enough for a good-bye cheer. But Garage had never won even half its games, and some of the players thought maybe it was the coaching. Joe never drilled them much in fundamentals, especially tactics, and teams like Car Wash, Pizza, and Footwear played rings around them on the field, passing and dribbling.

The other thing was that their jerseys were getting so faded from being washed that you could hardly read JOE'S GARAGE on the back or the numbers on the front. It made them feel a little crummy alongside some of the other teams in the league.

They also were using heavy, old-fashioned shin guards. It was up to the sponsor to supply uniforms and equipment. After all, he was getting the free advertising. Some members of the team had dropped a few hints, but it had done no good.

"Your new sponsor is going to be a lady," Joe told them now.

"A lady! You're kidding!"

"What lady?"

"The lady who has the new shop, across the Common, in the building where the garage was. Mary Louise."

"A lady sponsor?"

"Yes, and she'll be your coach, too."

"You've got to be kidding."

"I'm not. The Council approved her. She'll probably be down here and take over this Friday's practice."

"Here we go, down to last place."

"I'm quitting." That was Hughie.

"Did you say, 'Mary Louise'? Hey, Coach! Gregg hurt his knee. Come give it a kiss to make it better, Coach!" That was J.P. Hudson, always clowning around.

"What?" said Gregg, cocking his fist.

"Hey, quit! I didn't mean it. I didn't mean it," J. P. pleaded piteously.

"Why do you have to go to Hawaii, Joe?"

"What are they going to think, on the other teams, when they see we got some lady coaching us?"

No one had even thought about what the team would now be *called*—the new name they'd be wearing on the backs of their jerseys.

"It's going to work out just fine, believe me," Joe said. "I've got to go now. So long, guys."

"So long, Joe."

"Send us a postcard from the Islands."

"Right." And Joe was gone.

"What about it, Hughie? You going to quit?"

Hughie Digby was just looking grim. He wasn't talking.

7

Scrappy got the word almost first thing Thursday morning. She was working on her project for the Science Fair—speeding up mushroom growth with rock music. She kept the mushrooms inside a box, with a transistor radio playing around the clock, and was changing the batteries when J.P. Hudson came over and said, "You should have been to practice yesterday. Joe told us we're getting a new coach. It's a lady."

Scrappy looked as if she did not think she had heard correctly. She sounded confused. "Did Joe leave already?"

"Him and his wife are taking a plane this morning."

"I'm watching my mushrooms grow," Scrappy said.

"So now you're not the only female on the team."

"What lady?" Scrappy said. It was taking a lot of time for the idea to sink in.

"The lady who owns The Mary Louise Shop, across the Common. Mary Louise," J.P. explained.

"That lady is going to be the coach for Garage?"

"That's what Joe told us."

Scrappy seemed lost in thought, as she gazed at the mushrooms under the glass cover of the box. Finally she said, "I don't want to talk about it now. I'm busy. Good-bye."

J.P. looked pleased with himself and wandered back to his own project—mating a Japanese beetle with a black widow spider. So far, nothing had happened that J.P. could put in his report.

As the morning wore on, Scrappy gradually faced the truth—that Garage was going to have a lady coach. At noon, she ate her lunch in a hurry and walked across the Common to check things out. Of course she had noticed the new construction going up where the garage had been. It was a pretty building, made of old brick, with the store windows all in small, mullioned panes and with flower boxes on the windowsills. Very old-fashioned.

"Fastest construction I ever saw around here," Scrappy's father had said.

One of the shops already had its sign hung out— a board that swung from a fancy iron bracket and swayed just a little when the wind blew.

THE MARY LOUISE SHOP
Things for the Younger Set

Peeking through the open door, Scrappy saw that the store went far back and was stocked with all kinds of things for children, including stuffed pandas, lions, ducks, rabbits, frogs, koala bears, and other bedtime companions. She would have loved to pet the fuzzy gray fox curled up on a red satin pillow, at one side of the window. There was also a big, old-fashioned baby buggy and a bed with a canopy over it, trimmed with white lace. Above all else, Scrappy noticed the pretty dresses that were hanging on racks at many places in the store or were draped on the bed. Just the kind that Floramae Williams would love to wear, even at school.

Mary Louise was a slender, pretty woman with bright, soft-looking hair and blue eyes with long, dark lashes. She wore high-heeled shoes and a soft, airy dress that floated about her legs, as she moved from here to there, in the store. Scrappy could imagine her floating through the tall daisies, in slow motion, in a perfume commercial, or as someone in a fairy tale. All she needed was a wand with a lighted star on its tip, and Scrappy remembered the time, in second grade, when Floramae Williams was the Tooth Fairy in the Halloween play. If Mary Louise could scrunch herself back to when she was in the second grade, she probably would be just like Floramae Williams, wand and all.

Now when she spoke, her voice was like mint topping, Scrappy thought. "May I help you?" She was talking to Kevin's mother.

"No, I'm just looking."

"Do please look around. Make yourself at home."

Outside, Scrappy looked at the clothes displayed in the window and realized that the thing Floramae Williams had worn to school, the day before, must have come from The Mary Louise Shop—a fluffy little dress, soft with little blue roses on a pink background. Seeing her in that dress, during recess, she had dared Floramae to do a somersault on the rings —skin the cat.

"Oh, I'd never!" Floramae had gasped.

Now Scrappy took a last look at the furry gray fox on the red satin pillow in the window of The Mary Louise Shop, then turned her back on it and tromped back across the Common to school. "I've played my last game for Garage," she told herself. Garage was going to have a lady coach and that lady was Mary Louise, a grown-up Floramae Williams. The whole idea was outrageous. Scrappy could not even imagine that lady kicking a soccer ball, let alone telling her, Scrappy Bassett, how to do it.

"No way!" thought Scrappy. "Garage can deal me out. I'm not playing."

She had made her decision, and nothing was going to change it.

8

LEARN SELF DEFENSE
Kung Fu Made Easy

Learn this ancient martial art in one
week or your money back. Send
only three dollars plus fifty cents for
handling to the Apex Trading Company, Simpsonville, Ohio 43736,
and we will rush your Kung Fu
book to you by return mail.

Scrappy filled out the order form in the magazine,
enclosed three dollar bills and a piece of cardboard
with two quarters taped to it, then sealed the envelope and stuck on a stamp. "Daddy, will you please
mail this for me in San Francisco, on your way to
work?"

"Why don't you mail it in the post office, on your
way to school?"

"It's too slow, that way. Mail doesn't go out till
four o'clock."

"What's the big rush?" He looked at the address on the envelope. "What are you sending away for, this time?"

"Kung Fu lessons."

Her father gave her that long, questioning, partly amused look that she knew meant he thought she was weird but loved her anyway. "Who are you planning to overpower?" he asked.

"Nobody special. I'm quitting soccer. I have to do *something.*"

"You're not quitting soccer!"

"Yes, I am."

"What will Joe's Garage do without you?"

"The best they can."

"Why in the world are you quitting?"

"I'm not going to play on a team with a lady coach."

"A lady coach?"

"That's right."

"Who is the lady?"

"Mary Louise. She owns The Mary Louise Shop, down on the Common."

"You don't say."

"Did you ever see her?" asked Scrappy.

"As a matter of fact, yes. I've been in her shop."

"What did you buy?"

"Nothing. I was just looking around. She's very nice."

"As nice as Mother?" Scrappy had detected a certain note in her father's voice.

"Well, now, you're asking the wrong person a question like that," Mr. Bassett said. "No one's as nice as your mother. But Mary Louise comes close. You're changing the subject. Why can't you play on a team with a lady coach?"

"Because."

"What happened to Joe?"

"He went to Hawaii. He retired."

"Oh, of course, of course. And now the team's to be sponsored by The Mary Louise—" Scrappy's father cut himself short. Perhaps this wasn't the best time to remind his daughter of the whole, horrible truth—that the team was also going to get a new name. "Why don't you give Mary Louise a chance? She might be a good coach, even better than Joe. What do you say?"

"Daddy, am I really going to be a little . . . what I heard you say to mother?"

"What's that—a bandit?"

"You know what you said to Mother, that time."

"When?"

"Two weeks ago. You were talking to Mom. You said Scrappy was going to be a little *bleep*, just like her mother." Scrappy could not even bring herself to say the word.

"Ohhhhh. A little beauty. You weren't supposed to hear that."

"Well, I did. Am I?"

"The answer is—not if you keep a fierce, mean face on you, like you have at this moment, thinking mean thoughts about the new coach. I really have to call that discrimination of the worst kind. The very worst. You, of all people. Aren't you the one who thinks a girl can do anything a boy can do?"

"I don't care."

"When is your next practice?"

"Friday. But I'm not going."

"You should at least check her out."

"I'm not going."

"Then, I will go myself. Mary Louise deserves it. I'll get home from work early and drop in on practice. I'll bring you a full report."

"No! Don't! Don't bother. I'll do it."

"Hmmmmm?" said her father, again with that questioning look. "All right, then. See that you do."

"And don't forget to mail my letter, please. It's very important."

9

Keeping her promise to her father, Scrappy drifted over to the field, a little after five, that Friday afternoon and made herself invisible near the bleachers. There she merged with a half-dozen or so girls who were holding a big conference about which girl Stanley Perkins was in love with, and hoped that no one on the team would notice her. No one did—they were much too busy.

For once, the whole team had shown up at the very beginning of practice and was ready and waiting. Mary Louise came across the Common, just at five, not looking very much like a soccer coach. She had not had a moment in which to change out of her working clothes, except to slip into what looked like a brand-new pair of Adidas. In the past, Joe would be there ahead of time with five or six balls that he kept in a net bag, and a few members of the team would be there taking shots on goal or just fooling around. Mary Louise had arrived empty-handed.

"Hello, team," she said. "My name is Mary Louise."

A couple of kids muttered, "Hi," but otherwise it was spooky quiet.

"As I'm sure all of you know, by this time, I'm your new sponsor and your new coach. I expect to enjoy very much coaching you, and I hope you'll enjoy it, too. Also, I hope we win a lot of games, and I believe that we will."

No reaction.

"The reason I think so is because you all look like very good individual soccer players. I saw your last game, with Quality Cleaners."

"We got clobbered," somebody said.

"Four to zip."

"We're in sixth place."

"Never mind. All we need is a little more teamwork," she said. "Wait and see. Right now, will four boys come over to the shop with me and get some cartons? Also the bag of balls that Joe left with me."

Every boy volunteered. From where Scrappy stood, they looked awfully eager, and she wondered if they were going to act, around the new coach, the way they did around Floramae Williams—weird and silly. Mary Louise picked four and asked their names, promising to know the names of everyone on the team before two weeks had passed.

Those who remained could hardly wait to find out what might be in the cartons.

"It's got to be new jerseys."

"That would be neat."

"Will they be the same color as the old ones?"

"Color! The old ones aren't any color at all, anymore."

"New shin guards."

"Will there be cleats?"

"They're still against the rules."

Two minutes, and Mary Louise and her helpers were back on the field, carrying the bag of balls and four cartons between them.

"You may open the cartons, if you like," she said, as the team gazed upon them expectantly. They clawed the cartons open in a matter of seconds. Wild tigers could not have done it any faster. Out tumbled not only jerseys but shorts (dark blue, with a gold stripe down the side), crimson-banded knee-length socks, and superlight plastic shin guards. Whistles, wows, and cheers were heard as far away as the firehouse, as the team viewed the beautiful new uniforms.

Scrappy, still skulking near the bleachers, could not quite hear what everyone said, but she knew they were very excited. She was excited, herself, and was tempted to join the team right then and there. There was no question, as the jerseys were being unfolded and passed out, that they were a beautiful, bright crimson, with white lettering and numbers on them, front and back. Then, as some kids turned theirs inside out, she could see that they were reversible—crimson on one side and gold on the other, with black letters on the back and numbers on the front. This way, no matter what team you played against, you could be light or dark, depending on what color the other team was wearing. Quality Cleaners, Rumstead Motors, and one or two other clubs had reversible jerseys, and they were neat. They also helped a lot in practice scrimmage, when your own team was split up into two sides.

Now some of the kids had taken off their crummy old Joe's Garage jerseys and put on their new ones, and Scrappy could see for the first time that the old team name had become—she could hardly believe it —THE MARY LOUISE SHOP.

"Oh no! I don't believe it!" Scrappy groaned. This was too much. She had been a member of a team called Joe's Garage. It had always been Joe's Garage. Now, all of a sudden, what was it? Not only was Garage now being coached by a lady, but it wasn't even Garage, anymore. It was some boutique, in fact, the very same store where Floramae Williams' mother bought her stupid dresses. There was the name to prove it, right on the new jerseys, in gold letters—THE MARY LOUISE SHOP.

42

"Very definitely no way!" Scrappy decided. Would the rest of the team agree to wear those jerseys? How could they? Discouraged but not too surprised, she trudged over to the bicycle rack, unchained her bike and pedaled home. To please her father, she had checked everything out. Now all she hoped was that the Kung Fu lessons would not be too long in coming. Maybe, just maybe, Kung Fu could take the place of soccer in her life.

10

Next day in school Scrappy found out from Gregg and Kevin what happened after she left. In the first place, Mary Louise excused herself for having to leave early and promised it would not happen again. A full practice session would be held on Monday, same place, same time. The team had fooled around for a while, with a ball Mary Louise left with them on the promise that Gregg would be responsible for it and bring it to Monday's practice.

Pretty soon, a few kids hanging around the field began to notice the new jerseys and say things about them.

"Yoo-hoo, Mary Louise!" a boy called, in a high voice.

"Oh, Mary Loo-eeeeez! Don't kick the ball too hard!" another called out.

"This is it," thought Kevin. He was not too surprised.

Now a chorus of dumb cracks began to echo around the field. Members of the team imagined even more and worse remarks about the new name, and it wasn't long before, one after another, they were peeling off their new jerseys and getting back into the old ones, taking them out of the carton where they had tossed them.

Before long, practice began to break up, and Stu Patton called a meeting, over by the bicycle rack. "I don't know about any of you guys, but I'm not going to wear any jersey with that garbage on the back," Stu announced.

"Me neither."

"What do we do?"

"We can wear the old ones," Kevin said.

"These old rags?"

"These new jerseys are the neatest ones in the league. I mean, the color."

"You want to wear yours?"

"No."

"All this good stuff she gave us—it would be ungrateful not to wear the jerseys," Norris Collins said.

"We didn't ask for new jerseys. Not with that garbage on the back."

"The letters are sewed on. We can take them off."

"Can we?"

"Sure. Just use some scissors with sharp points and cut every stitch," Kevin explained. "Once I saw my mother take out stitches that way."

"That's a lot of work."

"You want to wear that silly name on your back?"

"No way."

"Okay, then. We rip it off."

"Maybe she wants to advertise her shop."

"Anyone knows that."

"I'm not any walking billboard."

"You were for Joe's Garage," Norris said.

"A garage is different."

"How about a dry cleaner?"

"That's different, too."

"How about a pizza parlor?"

"Shall we take a vote?" Stu Patton was getting impatient.

"Right," said Gregg.

The vote was unanimous for removing the letters before Monday's practice. It was one thing to go by the name of Car Wash or Concrete Mix. It was an entirely different matter to get tagged with Mary Louise.

That was how Scrappy heard it from Kevin and Gregg.

"That's not fair," she said. "You either play with the letters on your shirt or you don't play."

"How about you, Scrap?"

"I'm not playing. I'm into Kung Fu."

II

Monday at five, the new coach was out on the field with the bag of balls. She was wearing jeans, Adidas, and a Mary Louise Shop jersey, with the crimson side out. As the kids showed up on the field, a few at a time, looking both fractious and guilty in their new jerseys with nothing but nothing on the back, Mary Louise looked surprised for an instant, then very cool. During the entire practice, she never said one word about the missing letters. Did she figure that, if she said nothing, they would feel so ashamed that they would all sew the letters back on before the game that was coming up on Wednesday? If that's what she thought, she was partly right—they felt ashamed. But she was also partly wrong—no vote was taken to sew the letters back on.

"Gather round," she said and had them sit facing her in a semicircle, in front of the east goal. "Right at the beginning, I want to say that I think we have the stuff to win games and get right up there in the ratings. I understand that one of our good halfbacks is missing."

"Scrappy Bassett," Hughie volunteered.

"Well, never mind. We have plenty of talent. Your defense, in the game with Quality Cleaners, was fairly good. I saw that game. But we can't win games without scoring goals, so what do we need?"

"An attack," said Archie Davis. Archie played inside right.

"Right," said the coach. "Dribbling the ball all the way down the pitch by yourself is fine, but it's you alone against a lot of defenders, and it seldom scores goals. Remember that you have teammates. And when a defender meets you, don't try to get the ball past him all by yourself. Pass. Always know where an open teammate is, and pass it to him. Just a short pass. Just touch it, and it will reach him. Let's try it."

The coach split the squad into attackers and defenders. "Now, Defense, this isn't a scrimmage. We'll have a good scrimmage later. Right now, Defense, don't try to break up any passes by the attack. Just put yourself in their way and force them to pass. But allow them to make the passes and get the idea. Let them work the ball right down to where they can take a shot on goal. And goalie—that will be practice for you. What's your name?"

"Donald," said Donald Humbolt.

"Donald," she repeated, fixing the name in her mind. "All right, then, let's go."

This was going to be nothing like the way Joe had always coached them, if you could call what he did coaching. Joe just used to let them fool around, taking shots, practicing a little heading now and then, and taking corner kicks and penalty shots. Never any real teamwork. About the fourth time up and down the field, she said, "You're doing fine, but you're not leading with the ball. Always pass a little ahead of your man, so he gets it on the run and doesn't have to stop, to control the ball. Get it?"

By now, they were really puffing. But they kept on running and were moving the ball quite smoothly down the field, threading it back and forth between defenders.

"All right," she said finally. "Catch your breath. I'm sorry to say, I don't think you're in top condition. We'll have to do something about that. I'll take some laps around the field with you, after practice. And lay off the candy and the Cokes. Let me say, right now, in my book, the defense also attacks. Not only with long, clearing balls but with short passes to midfield players, when the chance comes. So let's turn it around, for a little while—the forward line defend. Fullbacks and halfbacks attack. Just for practice."

That's how it went until six o'clock, Mary Louise

telling them what they were doing wrong or doing right and even getting into the lineup, herself, to demonstrate. It was easy to see she had played a lot of soccer and must have been good.

At six, sharp, she said, "You're doing great, team. You're ready for Wednesday. On this field. Five o'clock."

"Pool Service," said Clark Unger.

"Right. Superior Pool Service versus—" She did not finish, just smiled a small, private smile. But everyone knew exactly what she was thinking—versus The Mary Louise Shop. "Not so fast, fellows," she said, as the team began to take off. "Three laps around the field before we're finished. Let's go."

That was the story Scrappy got, next day, from some boys on the team.

"So now, if she's so great, I guess you'll be sewing that stuff back on your jerseys," Scrappy said.

"I don't know," said Kevin. "But you should come back."

"No, thanks," said Scrappy. "I'm into the martial arts, from now on."

12

"Hey, Mom!" Scrappy shouted. "My Kung Fu book came! Why didn't you tell me?" Scrappy had found it on her desk, in her room, as she got home from school.

"Sorry," her mother said. "It only came in today's mail."

Scrappy did not answer. She was already into the book, which had surprised her by arriving just one week after she had given her father the letter to mail. Scrappy had sent away for things before and knew how long it usually took for them to arrive. The book had a paper cover and only about forty pages, most of them pictures. It wasn't worth fifty cents, let alone three dollars and fifty cents to cover handling and mailing. Still, if she could learn the ancient martial art of Kung Fu from it, it might be worth the money.

Scrappy began to read the book at four o'clock in the afternoon. At five o'clock, when her brother, Josh, parked his bicycle in the carport, he was met with a flurry of chops, kicks, and spins, accompanied by grunts and screams that made him sure his sister had at last gone totally bananas.

"Hold it, man! Hold it! Cool it!" he sputtered, as he finally subdued her with a headlock. Josh was a first-string running back on Redwood High's winning football team, weighed more than twice as much as his sister and was one foot taller. "What's got into you? What do you think you're doing?"

"Let go!" Scrappy squealed, struggling to escape.

"Do I dare? Is it safe?"

Scrappy stopped struggling, and Josh released his hold on her head. Scrappy gave him a rueful look and rubbed her ears, which smarted from being in the headlock.

"What was that all about?" Josh wanted to know.

"That's Kung Fu, stupid," Scrappy informed him. "It's an ancient martial art, and I'm learning it. I'm going to be a Black Belt. I'll lend you my book, and you can learn, too. Then you can fight fair. We can have bouts."

"Fight fair? I always fight fair."

"That wasn't fair, what you did. It wasn't Kung Fu. It was just ordinary rassling."

"It's good enough for me," Josh told her.

"You can borrow my book and learn the right way to do it."

52

"No thanks," said her brother. "I'm into the ancient art of meditation."

"You'll be sorry."

"I will?"

"With Kung Fu, a small person can subdue a large person who doesn't know it."

"I'll take my chances. I'm not a small person."

"You're mean. You're really mean."

"I know it," said Josh.

Scrappy hated him for at least a minute.

"How much more do you have to learn?" Josh asked.

"Twenty-one pages."

"And then you'll be a Black Belt?"

"Yes. But the last twenty-one pages are the hardest."

"Try me again, after you've finished the course. But no ambushing."

"Don't worry. I will. And will you be surprised."

"I hope so. I love surprises. So long. I have to study for at least an hour before dinner." He went inside, and Scrappy could hear him shut the door to his room and turn on his stereo.

Returning to her own room, Scrappy reviewed the first twenty pages of *Kung Fu Made Easy,* then came out into the hall and practiced the moves and grunts in front of the full-length mirror.

"Laura Jean Bassett!" It was her mother, who had come around out of the kitchen to see what was happening. "What are you doing? I thought we were having an earthquake." Some of the moves called for a lot of stomping and coming down hard on the soles of both feet at once. That way, even Scrappy's seventy-five pounds shook the house. "Stop it, now!"

"It's very important to know self-defense," Scrappy argued.

"Defense! That sounded more like attack," her mother said.

"That's part of it. To psych out the attacker."

"Well, please psych the attacker out more quietly, if you don't mind." Sometimes her mother failed to understand the simplest things.

Scrappy's father usually drove into the driveway at a quarter after six. This evening, at ten after, Scrappy was lurking in the carport, ready to pounce. Mr. Bassett arrived at exactly a quarter after, got out of the car, carrying his briefcase, and started for the door. This was her chance.

Suddenly something kept Scrappy from launching her attack. Her father looked fragile and easy to hurt. The thought of hurting him almost made her cry. "Hello, Daddy," she said, walking up to him and exchanging hugs.

"Why, hello, Scrap. How nice of you to meet

me out here. What have you been doing?"

"Nothing much. Only learning Kung Fu."

'Oh, did the book come? So soon?"

"It came. But there's no one to fight. I offered to teach Josh, but he could care less about the martial arts."

"Do you have to fight someone? Can't you just practice the art of self-defense by yourself."

"What fun is that? I guess I just wasted my money."

"I suppose I could learn," said Mr. Bassett.

"No! You're too skinny. You might get hurt."

"You don't say! I'll thank you to remember that I ski the Devil's Drop, at Bald Mountain, without mishap."

"That's different. Anyway, girls don't fight with their fathers."

"It seems to me that someone else in school must have sent away for *Kung Fu Made Easy*. Have you checked around?"

"No. I never thought of that. I'll do it tomorrow."

"By the way, what happened to soccer?" her father asked.

"Oh, that," said Scrappy.

"Oh, yes," her father remembered. "The lady coach. To think we've raised a female chauvinist piglet."

"What's that?" Scrappy wanted to know.

"Your mother will tell you. Any idea of what we're having for dinner?"

"Uh-uh."

Together they went inside and began to sniff for telltale smells from the kitchen.

13

Next day in school, Scrappy let it be known subtly that she now was a student of the ancient martial art of Kung Fu. She placed her book on her chair arm, where everyone could see it, and between subjects and activities practiced Kung Fu moves in slow motion and with soft grunts and snorts. Her teacher gave her a few curious glances, and some of the kids made a wide circle around her when they passed her. But everyone politely avoided saying anything about her strange behavior. It was very frustrating.

Finally, of all people in the room, Floramae Williams came over to Scrappy and said, "Where do you take?"

"Where do I take what?" Scrappy asked.

"Kung Fu."

"Kung Fu?" She was so surprised that she hardly understood the question. Was taking Kung Fu something like taking ballet or flute now?

"Yes. Where do you take?"

"I don't take anywhere. I'm learning out of a book. Did you ever hear of it?" A dumb question, Scrappy realized, considering the question Flora-mae had just asked her.

"I take every Wednesday, after school, at the Red-wood Health and Fitness Center," Floramae said. "Kung Fu for mothers and daughters. My mother takes, too. We take together."

Scrappy looked blank, as if she had just gone over the handlebars of her bike and was lying on the ground, thinking about getting up.

"Women need to know self-defense, these days," Floramae explained.

Pulling herself together, Scrappy said, "I never defend myself. I only attack." What she said made no sense, but it was the best she could think of, at the moment. She had been trying to find someone to fight her in Kung Fu. Now she had found some-one. None other than Floramae Williams, prettiest girl in the class, now wearing a dress right out of The Mary Louise Shop collection, the last kind of girl in the whole world Scrappy Bassett wanted to be—or to fight—now taking Kung Fu from a real Kung Fu teacher, probably a Black Belt. Mothers and daughters. "Good luck," said Scrappy and took *Kung Fu Made Easy* up to the front of the room and dropped it in the wastebasket. Three dollars and fifty cents down the tubes.

Later, when no one was looking, thinking better of the matter, she fished it out. Since she'd paid for the book, she might as well finish the course. Who could know? She might have occasion to use the martial arts someday.

14

Scrappy Bassett was standing on the post office steps scanning the village billboard, which was stuck full of posters and announcements of everything from volunteer house sitters to the Shakespearean Fair, which had been over for three weeks. Finding the weekly list of the soccer standings for the nine teams in the county, she saw that the crimson No Names, formerly Joe's Garage, already had come up from sixth to fifth, after only four games under the new coach. This was not exactly news to Scrappy. Six members of the team were in her room at school, and that was almost all they ever talked about, to each other or to Scrappy—when she would listen, which was hardly ever.

"I will never watch another soccer game." That had been Scrappy Bassett's solemn vow, when she resigned from the team. But could she keep that vow? Especially now that Kung Fu gave such little promise of taking the place of soccer in her life. Right now, across the Common from the post office, two teams were warming up—Pizza, in bright green jerseys, and Scrappy's old team, in crimson. As she stood there, the whistle blew and the game was on. Suddenly it was as if someone else was controlling Scrappy's feet, which half-strolled, half-skipped across the Common to the soccer field, carrying their owner unwillingly to a position beside the bleachers. There she managed to make herself invisible in the shadow of Kirsten Caldwell, who was only in Scrappy's class but was quite large.

Almost at once, Scrappy could see why the crimsons had been winning games. No crimson jersey ever risked losing the ball to a tackler, but found an open man and passed it to him, the instant he was challenged. That way, they kept working the ball down to Pizza's goal and taking shots, and only the great Pizza goalie kept it from being a slaughter. Pizza had good individual players, but they didn't pass enough and kept losing the ball back to the crimsons before they could get close enough to the crimson goal to take a shot. That's what the guys had meant by teamwork, when they told Scrappy about it. Right now, every time Hughie or Todd or one of the wingmen took a shot, one of Scrappy's feet would give a violent twitch and kick an imaginary ball so hard that the Pizza goalie would never even have seen it as it roared past his ears. Just standing there and watching was horrible torture. She never should have come.

As tactics on the field brought different players near where Scrappy was lurking, they called out to her.

"How you doing, Scrappy? How's Kung Fu?"

"You should be in uniform, Scrappy. Why don't you suit up?"

"Hey, Scrappy! You ought to be out here. We need you."

"Hey, Scrappy! Stop trying to hide!"

"We see you, Scrappy!"

By twelve minutes into the game, the crimson jerseys were up two goals to zip against Pizza, who up to now stood third in the league. Then the crimsons and Pizza each got a goal, and the half ended three to one, crimsons.

The game ended with another score each for the crimsons and Pizza, which made it four to two, crimsons. They had beaten the third best team in the league, and where did that put them? Kevin Garvey's mother had taken out her computer and was working it out.

"You can't do it, Mrs. Garvey," Candice Dobbs said. "Not unless you know who else won or lost today."

"Were there other games?" Mrs. Garvey asked.

"Three."

"Oh, well," said Mrs. Garvey. "Our team had to at least stay in fifth. It couldn't go down."

"I bet it went up," said Scrappy. That is what she hoped. Suddenly, whether she realized it or not, she felt very loyal to Garage or whatever they called it now. After all, it was her team. She had played left halfback for it once. Suddenly she was wondering if the team would take her back, especially the coach. What if she knew that Scrappy had quit because of her? Maybe she ought to at least find out when next practice was. Maybe she'd come out. Those crimson jerseys looked awfully pretty to her, not to mention the new shin guards that hardly showed at all under the socks. As long as Mary Louise was a good coach, Scrappy didn't suppose it would hurt her just to be on the team. She didn't even have to talk to Mary Louise, if she didn't want to.

"Hi, Hughie," she said, as the center forward strode past her on his way to the drinking fountain.

"Oh, hi, Scrappy."

"When's the next practice?"

"Friday, at five. Are you coming?"

"I have to decide." Actually there was little doubt in Scrappy's mind that she would be there. She had practically decided.

15

That night at dinner, just before dessert, Mrs. Bassett made an announcement. Tapping lightly on her glass to emphasize the special importance of her message, she said, "Your brother Mike phoned, this morning, to tell us that he is engaged and is going to be married in less than one month."

Scrappy looked around at her father and brother, Josh, to see if they were as surprised as she was—and as startled. They weren't. They just smiled, and Scrappy knew that they already had heard the news and that her mother had been saving it for just the right time to tell her. Just before dessert must have seemed the right time.

"That's all right with me," Scrappy said. "He can get married anytime he wants to."

"I'm glad you approve," said her father.

"Who's he engaged to?" Scrappy asked.

"You know very well who he's engaged to," her mother said. "What a silly question."

"Pam?" asked Scrappy.

"Naturally," said Josh, not sounding the least bit natural.

"Is Pam all right with you?" her father asked.

"Why not?" said Scrappy.

"You know you love Pam," said her mother. "She's a darling girl. Mike's very lucky."

"What's the big rush for the wedding?" Josh asked.

"That's what I say," said Scrappy.

"Mike has a teaching fellowship, back in Wisconsin, right after graduation. That's the other news. Naturally they want to get married before they go away."

"How far is Wisconsin?" Scrappy wanted to know.

"Far enough," said Josh. "They won't be coming home every weekend or so. That's for sure."

"Oh," said Scrappy. This was a lot of news for her to take in all at once, even at the best of times. She always loved it when her brother came home for a weekend. Now she was hardly ever going to see him. She swallowed hard and looked grim. Her mother looked as if she had still more news. If she did, she was saving it until later. That was all right with Scrappy. She had heard enough.

Later that evening, Scrappy's mother said, "How

would you like to be a junior bridesmaid at your brother's wedding?"

"What's that?" Scrappy asked. She had a feeling that this was going to be the rest of the bad news.

"Oh, I think you have a pretty good idea. After all, you attended your cousin Kathy's wedding, last fall, and saw just what happened. You will walk in the wedding procession, just behind the bridesmaids, with one other young girl. It's going to be outdoors, in a beautiful park, down at Santa Barbara. You will carry a bouquet, and of course you will wear a pretty dress." Having said this, Mrs. Bassett held her breath.

"A dress!" Scrappy exclaimed. "That's really weird. I won't do it."

"Your brother and Pam are very anxious to have you. They especially told me."

"I won't wear a dress."

"You'll look awfully funny, the only member of the wedding in blue jeans."

Scrappy was silent. If her brother wanted her to be something at his wedding, then she wanted to be it. But to wear a dress—that was asking too much. The very thought caused Scrappy to panic. A pretty dress! Floramae Williams! Yech!

"I'll meet you right after school tomorrow, and we'll go shopping."

"Tomorrow afternoon is soccer practice."

"Oh, are you playing soccer again?"

"Yes." She had just decided, definitely—at that exact moment.

"What happened to Kung Fu?"

"Who needs it?"

"I see." Sometimes it did not do to ask Scrappy for explanations. "What time is practice?"

"Five."

"We'll be finished shopping by five. I shouldn't be surprised if the new store, right on the Common, had exactly what you need."

"The Mary Louise Shop?"

"That's right. It's a lovely store."

Scrappy groaned. It had been an unlucky day for Scrappy, all around, when Joe's Garage had decided to close its doors on Bagley Common.

16

Next day, after school, Scrappy met her mother at the post office. After a friendly chat with Roger Fuller's mother, who always came for her mail on a bicycle, Mrs. Bassett said, "Let's go, dear. And please stop looking grim. Nothing terrible is going to happen to you."

"How do I know that?" thought Scrappy.

It was only a very short walk to The Mary Louise Shop, but for Scrappy every step seemed a step closer to the end. She would probably have to try on a lot of dresses before they bought one. "I wish we were going to the dentist," Scrappy said.

"Good afternoon," said Mary Louise.

"We're looking for a long dress," Scrappy's mother said. "Scrappy is going to be a junior bridesmaid at her brother's wedding."

"Oh, is this Scrappy? Scrappy Bassett?"

"Her real name is Laura Jean," her mother said. She never had altogether approved of "Scrappy."

"I've heard a great deal about you, Scrappy," Mary Louise said.

Scrappy wondered what the team had been saying about her.

"A long dress. Any particular color?"

"Any pale pastel color. The wedding's to be out of doors."

"I think I may have exactly what you want." Mary Louise went to a rack and took down a dress that Scrappy thought could be stuffed into a lunch box with room left over for a sandwich and a banana. The dress was pale pink and was made of filmy material, all puckered and frilled. Mary Louise held it up against Scrappy and said, "Would you like to try this one on?"

The look on Scrappy's face said a definite *no*.

"I think it might be just the thing," said her mother. "We'll need a petticoat, of course."

"Of course," said Mary Louise. Taking a pale pink one out of a drawer, she said, "This one should go very nicely with the dress."

"Oh, no!" thought Scrappy. "One dress under another."

"Right over here," said Mary Louise.

Scrappy's Adidas seemed planted in the carpet, but her mother, undaunted, steered her daughter into the little dressing room to which Mary Louise had directed them. "Please take off your jeans and T-shirt," said Mrs. Bassett. Scrappy obeyed, and her mother dropped the soft sacks over her head.

Scrappy felt trapped, and she felt sorry for butter-flies caught in nets. Her mother tugged and pulled and smoothed down the material and said, "There! Let's go out there and see how you look." They went out into the main part of the shop, and Mary Louise led Scrappy toward a mirror that was taller than she was.

"Let me see what I can do with your hair," her mother said and slipped off the rubber band that held it in a pony tail. Scrappy could feel it fall around her ears in loose curls.

"She looks darling," Mary Louise said. But Scrappy had kept her eyes tightly closed. Except for one tiny, fuzzy glimpse, she had no idea of how she looked and did not want to know. Suppose she liked the way she looked in the dress. What might happen? She might turn gradually, even suddenly, into a Floramae Williams, the way a butterfly emerges from a cocoon. Even now, the soft, light stuff hanging from her shoulders and against her legs gave her a certain feeling that she liked—and that scared her. The way Floramae Williams and Elaine Sorenson and probably Mary Louise, herself, must feel—with her soft-looking hair and blue eyes and smile that looked like a commercial for toothpaste. It must be the way Floramae felt all the time and loved to feel —scared of the playground trapeze rings, squealing with terror at a slug in a jar, making boys act silly and weird around her. Lurid. Scrappy tried to concentrate on Kung Fu moves she had learned from the book, just as she always concentrated on burros at the dentist. If her brother wanted her to be a junior bridesmaid, she would be one. But she would not like it. She was determined to suffer hard, every minute she had to wear the petticoat and the dress.

"Would you care to look at some others?" Mary Louise said.

"I think not," said Scrappy's mother. "I think this one will do very nicely. Let's not push our luck," she added quietly.

"Of course. Just let me wrap it up for you."

Scrappy could see that Mary Louise was being extra nice to her mother, because she couldn't wait to sell the dress and get the money for it and put it in the bank. What a waste of money!

"Are we going to see you out for the team again, Scrappy?" Mary Louise asked, as Mrs. Bassett wrote out the check to pay for the dress.

Scrappy said nothing, just stared at her Adidas, set stubbornly in the thick carpet that covered the shop floor. She could tell that her mother and Mary Louise exchanged knowing glances, but it made no difference. She was having nothing to do with this lady with soft hair and long eyelashes and a dress that floated and swished around her legs when she walked—who had sold her mother the dress she would have to wear at her brother's wedding, who had put her store where Joe's Garage used to be, so that the team wasn't Garage anymore but The Mary Louise Shop, even if the name wasn't on the jerseys. She wasn't going to play on that team. That was final.

"We'd like to have you," Mary Louise was saying. "I understand you're a very good shooter."

Scrappy closed her eyes and imagined booting one in past the Pizza goalie.

"Well, thank you for coming in," said Mary Louise. "I hope we'll be seeing you again before too very long."

"Oh, I wouldn't be surprised," Mrs. Bassett said, and the way she said it made Scrappy feel as though her mother and Mary Louise and every grown-up in the world, including her brother, Mike, but maybe not her father, was in a plot against her.

Outside, Scrappy said, "Please put the rubber band back on my hair."

"Of course, dear," her mother said. "If that is really the way you want to look."

17

"What am I doing here?" Scrappy asked herself. She was in a hotel room in the seaside town of Santa Barbara, where she could see the Pacific Ocean from one window, if she stood on a chair. "Here I am getting ready to put on this silly dress. My hair is hanging down and all curly. I'm getting ready to help my brother get married so he won't belong to our family anymore but to Pam. I hate Pam. No I don't. I just hate her taking Mike away. Bleep!"

The only good thing about the wedding was that her cousin Rick was going to be there, the one who told her she looked like a seal coming up for a fish. Rick was fourteen now. He was three years older than Scrappy. Always had been, as far back as she could remember, and always would be, no matter how old she got. But he had always been nice to her. Now he was here for the wedding, but she had had a chance only to say hello to him, so far, what with the rehearsal that morning. Rick had always been big for his age, very grown-up. This morning he had seemed even older than fourteen and was very good looking in his blue blazer, white shirt, and red and blue striped tie. She hoped that later he would come over and talk to her.

Right now, Scrappy's mother was dropping the dress over her head, pulling it down, straightening it, tying the bow at the back. It was the only time Scrappy had tried it on since the day at the store, except once when her mother had made it a little longer.

Her mother gave her hair a little touch with the brush and said, "Just look at yourself now. You look darling." She turned Scrappy around to face the mirror on the bathroom door. Not once until this moment had she looked at herself in a mirror in her junior bridesmaid's dress. Scrappy was startled. The girl in the mirror was prettier than any picture she had ever seen, even in a magazine. She was just as pretty as Floramae Williams or Elaine Sorenson. That girl in the mirror was really cute, and Scrappy loved her. But who was it? It couldn't be Scrappy. Scrappy didn't look like that. She moved her left hand a little, then her right. So did the girl in the mirror. She made her Bugs Bunny face. The girl in the mirror showed her top two incisors. Astonished, she turned to her mother.

"Is that me?" Scrappy asked.

"Do you like her?"

Scrappy just took a very deep breath and let it out.

"Yes, it certainly is you," her mother assured her.

A wave of enchantment swept over Scrappy Bassett.

"You never imagined you could look so pretty, did you?"

"I look like that?"

"You certainly do. Your brother will be very proud of his little sister. Not so little, either. Quite a young lady."

That was another thing. The long dress made her look tall and old. The way her hair was fixed made her look grown-up. Scrappy stared at her reflection, and her reflection stared back. Slowly, very slowly, as she stared, she became anxious, then alarmed. What was going on here? What was she turning into? Was she turning into something completely different from Scrappy Bassett—the thing her father had said? Floramae Williams was a little beauty. Everyone knew that. Hi, Floramae. Want to pet my slug? Eek! Oh, sorry. Was Scrappy turning into something helpless? Afraid of slugs and spiders? Stuck up? Someone who took Kung Fu with her mother, for self-defense? Was she turning into something boys would begin to act silly about and treat like a girl? Could a girl like that ever play soccer again on a boys' soccer team? Would she even *want* to? Oh, wow! Panic time!

"Please turn all the way around once," her mother said. "I want to see you."

Scrappy spun around. The soft fabric whispered against her. It felt delicious.

"How does it feel on you?"

Suddenly, no sound would come out of Scrappy.

"How does it feel, Scrappy?"

"I . . . don't . . . know," Scrappy managed to say.

"Well, is it comfortable?"

Comfortable? Does a keg of gunpowder feel comfortable with its fuse sputtering? Scrappy felt explosive. She felt only seconds from blowing up, with a terrible bang, and blowing everyone and everything near her right over the treetops. *That kid is dynamite.* That's what her father had said when she was little. Now it was the truth. She felt like a bomb made in the shape of a girl and wearing a long pale pink dress with a bow in back.

"It's time to go now, dear," her mother was saying. "And you be good."

Good? What else had her mother been saying? She had no idea.

"Your flowers will be given you when you get there. You and Josh will go in our car. Daddy will drive."

Josh was an usher and was wearing a dark blue suit with shiny lapels and collar and a pale purple shirt with ruffles up the front and on the cuffs. He looked to Scrappy as if he must feel ridiculous.

Scrappy got into the car in a daze and remained in a daze all the way to the park.

18

The place in the park where the wedding was to take place was a grassy glade that sloped gently toward a small stream. Tall, spreading trees at each side and at the bottom of the slope provided shade on this hot, still day. Down near the stream was a small stone altar, for people who liked to be married out of doors. Nearby were picnic tables, where right now refreshments were being set out for the wedding guests. At the top of the slope, where Scrappy was waiting with other members of the wedding, she could see her brother down near the altar. With him were the minister, the best man, who had the ring in his pocket, and three other college friends, who were ushers. All but the minister now were dressed up like Josh, in weird suits and shirts. Scrappy had met them all at rehearsal, in the morning. Then everyone, even the minister and Pam, was wearing jeans. Two ushers were up near the parking place, telling the guests where to go. But most just drifted down the slope to be near the altar and hear the music, which was being made by two men and a girl, singing and playing guitars. They, too, were college friends of Mike's.

At the top of the slope, waiting for the wedding to start, was the bride with her attendants, including Scrappy. The other junior bridesmaid, younger than Scrappy but as tall, was named Marjorie. She was Pam's niece. Scrappy had never seen her until the rehearsal that morning, and she tried to figure out if now Marjorie was going to be a new relative of some kind. Her dress was very light blue and just as clinging and soft-looking as Scrappy's.

"You two girls look like a pair of little peonies," said a lady who probably was somebody's aunt.

"What are peenees?" Marjorie asked Scrappy.

"Flowers," said Scrappy, unhappily.

"Oh," said Marjorie.

Beside the parking lot were some steep, rugged rocks, put there for only one purpose—to be climbed. Never mind her white patent leather shoes and her junior bridesmaid's dress, the rocks beckoned to Scrappy and she started toward them.

"Don't get too far away, Scrap," an usher cautioned her. He was the one, named Ross, whom she had met that morning. It was his job to give the signal for the start of the wedding procession, up near the parking lot, at the top of the slope. "We're liable to start any minute now," he warned her.

"Okay," said Scrappy, as she took off for the rocks. She had just gotten a good toehold in a crevice when she noticed her cousin, Rick, who had joined some wedding guests at the other side of the lot. He had just arrived, Scrappy supposed, or she would have seen him. She climbed a little higher, to a flat-topped rock, stood up straight and raised her right arm, like the Statue of Liberty. Rick saw her and waved carelessly and went on talking. What if he didn't recognize her, all dressed up like this? She felt disappointed, then suddenly excited, as she thought of how surprised he might be when he realized who it was. Maybe he would even treat her as if she were grown-up—twelve or thirteen, at least, instead of merely just turned eleven. In her long dress, she felt almost grown-up. It was a strange feeling and just a little scary. A light breeze was blowing in from the ocean. It was rustling the eucalyptus leaves and blowing the girls' summer dresses. High up where she was, Scrappy felt the soft material of her petticoat blowing against her knees. The feeling was touchy-tingly and very nice, and she wondered if Floramae Williams felt this way whenever the wind blew.

Standing on the high rock, Scrappy's thoughts floated off in all directions, finally homing in on her room at Bagley Elementary, where so many things went on, besides subjects. "T.N. loves F.W." she was thinking. Everyone knew that. Todd Nelson was supposed to be the best-looking boy in the room. Could Scrappy make T.N. love S.B., if she wanted to? Not that she wanted to, but *could* she, now that she knew she was as pretty as Floramae Williams? Would she have to do something special, or was it enough just to be pretty? Would she have to wear dresses all the time instead of jeans and let her hair hang down loose and curly? It was all very mysterious and interesting to think about, atop the rock.

In spite of the breeze, it was warm, and Scrappy was thirsty. She decided to get a drink at the fountain at the far corner of the parking lot. Scrambling down from her lookout, she strolled across the lot. She had not gone far when she saw Rick move away from his friends and walk toward the fountain himself. "He left them to come to me," she said to herself, feeling pleased. He was looking directly at her.

"Hi, Scrappy!" he called.

How big and old he looked, and how very nice. Compared to Rick, Todd Nelson was a mere child. Scrappy wondered what Floramae Williams would do, if she met Rick. Could she make him act strange and weird, if she wanted to? She wondered what she, herself, could do to fluster Rick just a little, maybe make him blush. Rick was close enough now, as he strolled toward the fountain, for her really to see his eyes. They were dark brown and very pretty —she had forgotten. Close enough to see the expression on his face. He was looking at her now in a way she never had seen him look at her before—surprised. Confused. Maybe a little bit stunned. Definitely weird. Then Scrappy knew that she, herself, must be doing it—whatever *it* was that Floramae Williams did—doing it to Rick, as they drew together at the drinking fountain.

"Gross!" Scrappy thought, and a hot wave of embarrassment washed over her. It was a word she never, ever used, except for the grossest things she could think of and nothing else—like stealing stuff from stores and keeping a rabbit in a very small cage for ever and ever. "I am being gross." Somehow, she never thought that Floramae Williams was gross, making boys act that way—merely strange. Floramae Williams was just being herself. For Scrappy, it seemed different. Why? She did not know. She knew only that she felt yechy. She wanted to dry up and blow away that very second.

Instead, she just kept walking toward the drinking fountain, and so did Rick, until they were face to face. By this time, Rick did not look quite so weird, not so surprised and baffled. He was merely smiling his beautiful, wide smile and taking Scrappy in, from head to toe.

"Hi," Scrappy said. "Have a drink."

"Ladies first," said Rick.

"Huh?" said Scrappy.

"Go ahead, Laura Jean. Take a drink." Sometimes he called her by her regular name, and she did not know whether she liked it or not. It seemed some kind of little joke with him, but not as if he were making fun of her. At least, she wasn't sure. She took a drink, and when she stood up and wiped her mouth with the back of her hand, she said, "Now, you."

Instead of taking his turn, Rick just looked at her for a moment in a curious way, without saying a thing.

"What's the matter?" said Scrappy. "Aren't you thirsty?"

"You look awful cute," Rick said. "You know that? Hey! I'm going to call you Barbie Doll from now on."

"What?" said Scrappy, turning to him sharply.

"From now on, I think I'll just call you—"

Rick never got the chance to repeat what he had said. Scrappy took one step toward him and landed a karate chop alongside his ear that caught him off balance and sent him staggering backward, sprawling on the grass behind the drinking fountain. For about two seconds, Scrappy stood over him, as if she had just won the Kung Fu championship of the world. At that instant, a ref's whistle sounded shrilly and the starting usher's voice was heard loud and clear, announcing that the wedding procession was about to begin. Leaving her victim still flat on his back, with a look of wild bewilderment on his face, Scrappy scurried to take her place as a junior bridesmaid in the wedding procession. Not a single guest had noticed the short, one-sided battle.

"All right, everyone! Everyone in their places!" The starting usher held a handkerchief high and brought it down sharply. The guitar music and the singing came to an end, down by the altar, and a wedding march began to come from hidden speakers somewhere up in the trees. "All right, go!" he commanded.

Four ushers, walking two by two, went first. Next came four bridesmaids, Pam's friends, also in pairs. Then all by herself came the maid of honor. Following her came the two junior bridesmaids, Scrappy and Marjorie. Bringing up the rear, eight paces behind, was the bride, her hand on the arm of her father, Dr. Hampton, who was going to give her away to Scrappy's brother. Would Mike own her then, Scrappy wondered. Right then she made up her mind that, if she ever had to be owned by somebody, she would never get married. Down the long slope toward the altar they all marched, taking slow steps to the slow music. Scrappy kept her eyes mostly on her white patent leather shoes, which she had scuffed up, climbing on the rocks. Those feet, out of Adidas, did not even look to Scrappy like her own. And as she walked, coming closer to the altar, stride by stride, her petticoat felt softer and silkier than ever, and her hair hung soft and fluffy around her ears. Scrappy liked these new, exciting feelings. In fact, she loved them. But something was different. Something quite remarkable had come over Scrappy. Suddenly she did not *care* what kind of delicious feelings her clothes stirred up in her. Why should she care? Whatever Scrappy might be turning into—a little beauty, as her father had predicted, even as pretty a girl as Floramae Williams, with just as much mysterious power to make boys act weird and silly about her, if she cared to, even a boy as old as her cousin, Rick—whatever was happening to her, she still was Scrappy, *and she knew it!* Scrappy Bassett, Kung Fu battler supreme. Scrappy Bassett, left halfback on a boys' soccer team. Right! With a lady coach! She made her decision to play, once and for all. So bring on first-place Shoe Store and their great goalie, Taggart. Bring on the junior Kung Fu champion of North America. Bring on a whole jar of slugs and a carton of spiders. Bring on the trapeze rings, too. Hey, this was a park, wasn't it! Maybe they had rings here! Hey! Maybe she'd skin the cat —in her long dress.

The music stopped. She had reached the place where she and the other peony were supposed to stand while her brother and Pam got married by the minister. Looking back up the slope, she tried to find her cousin but could not see him. She hoped he was all right. She had let him have it with everything she had.

19

From where Scrappy stood, as a member of the wedding, she could hear every word everyone said—the minister, her brother, and Pam—and could see their faces. Pam and the minister looked very serious, but she thought her brother was having trouble keeping from breaking out into his widest, most beautiful grin. She hoped he would. She even tried to catch his eye, to make her Bugs Bunny face. That would break him up, if anything would. But he kept his eyes fixed firmly on the minister, except when he glanced at Pam. Scrappy understood that her brother and Pam had made up their own words for the marriage ceremony, but she was not thinking much about what they were saying. Mostly she was thinking that her brother and Pam were going to live in some other state, and she would hardly ever see them.

"I'll never get married," Scrappy told herself, but she knew in her heart that she probably would, someday. All girls got married, especially if some-one thought they were pretty.

The bride and groom kissed, and it was over. Suddenly Scrappy felt starved, from all the excitement, and wanted to dash down to the refreshment tables, which she had checked out earlier.

"Not so fast, Scrappy," her father said. "Let's congratulate your brother and new sister-in-law."

That is what everyone was doing, and when her turn came, Scrappy said, "Congratulations." Pam and Mike each hugged her, and Mike lifted her off her feet when he did it. Relatives, who had come down from San Francisco, greeted her and said she had grown and was quite a young lady. Two college friends of Mike's, who had come home for a week-end with him once, said, "Hi-yah, Scrappy. How you doing?" Most of the wedding guests were strangers. Still, several of them smiled at her in a friendly way, as if they thought she was nice, and a lady with red hair said she thought Scrappy made a lovely junior bridesmaid. She smiled at the lady—not her Bugs Bunny smile but a real smile that went with feeling happy, which was how she felt, right then, except for thinking about food and wondering if she would see Rick again before they left. Right now, he was nowhere in sight. Would he speak to her, if he saw her, or would he think she was too weird? But she wasn't sorry for what she had done to him—she had to do it. Barbie Doll? *Uh-uhhh!*

At last, when no one was paying any attention to her, she slipped away, walking slowly at first, then dashing toward the refreshments. Even at that, she was not the first one there. Making a choice from among the good things spread out on the tables was so impossible that she did not even try, just took one of everything excepting an egg salad and cucumber sandwich. There wasn't room for it on her plate, and she could always come back and get one later. Setting her plate on the corner of the table, she bit off half a brownie, helped herself from the children's punch bowl, then went to work in earnest on her plateful of food. She was swallowing the second half of the brownie and biting into a macaroon when she saw Rick strolling down toward the tables.

Seeing her, he halted for an instant, then approached cautiously. Scrappy tried to say, "Hi," but the greeting got stuck somewhere between the brownie and the macaroon, and nothing came out.

"Don't try to talk with your mouth full," Rick said, from a safe distance.

Scrappy took a gulp of the pink punch and said, "Pardon me," then gulped again and said, "Hi. I'm very sorry I hit you. I hope it didn't hurt when you landed."

"Hurt? Oh no, nothing like that. Where did you ever learn that chop to the jugular?"

"That was on page eleven in *Kung Fu Made Easy.*"

"What did I say that made you do a thing like that? What did I do?"

"It wasn't your fault. It's too hard to explain."

"Girls!" Rick said. "They are weird."

"I know," said Scrappy.

"Well, you do look cute in that dress, with your hair curled," he said, very seriously but ready to beat a retreat.

"It isn't curled. It's natural."

"Anyway, you look very nice."

"I don't care if I do," said Scrappy, merrily. "Would you care for some Shirley Temple?"

"Why not?" Rick said, and she dipped him out a cup of the pink liquid, making sure that he got a cherry in it.

20

Sunday, at the wedding, Scrappy had made her big decision—go out for soccer again. After all, she wanted so much to play that it almost hurt, just thinking about it. Playing for The Mary Louise Shop couldn't be all bad. Mary Louise was a great coach, no doubt about it, and the dress from her shop hadn't turned Scrappy into anything strange or weird, at least not yet.

"Scrappy Bassett at left halfback," she was saying to herself. That was on Sunday.

Monday night, after dinner, back home in Bagley, Mrs. Bassett remarked, "I'm sorry to hear that The Mary Louise Shop will be closing. Isn't that a shame?"

"I'm not surprised," Mr. Bassett said. "It seems to be the fate of most small stores that start up around here."

Scrappy suddenly paid attention. "Why is it closing?" she asked.

"Not enough people come into the store, I suppose," her father said. "She doesn't sell enough to make it pay."

"Oh," said Scrappy.

Talk at the table already had turned to other things when Scrappy said, "Maybe she should advertise a whole lot, so people would know about it and come there to buy."

"Are we talking about Mary Louise again?" her father asked.

"Yes," said Scrappy.

"Advertising costs money. She probably can't afford to advertise."

"Oh," said Scrappy. Her mind was doing somersaults and flips. "Will the team get another new sponsor, after she leaves?"

"Very likely," said her mother. "A good team has great value to a business."

"Like who?" Scrappy wondered.

"Might be Elite," said her father. "I understand they're looking for a team."

"Elite what?" asked Josh, with a mischievous grin. He knew the answer.

"Elite Garbage Collection," said Mr. Bassett.

"Huuuuuuh?" said Scrappy, beginning to see it all—spelled out in large letters on the team's jerseys.

"Huuuuuuh?" she exclaimed again, as it all sunk in. "Eeeee-yech! Not that!"

Tuesday morning, at exactly eleven-seventeen, in the middle of changing the batteries in her mushroom experiment, Scrappy decided that there was no way she now could go back on her decision, made at the wedding, to go out for soccer, no matter what happened. Still, this was a situation with no future that she could see.

Hi, Scrappy—how's Garbage doing in the ratings?

Yea-a-a-a-ay, Garbage! Way to go, Garbage!

C'm o-o-o-on . . . Scrappy! Let's see you score for Garbage!

Two, four, six, eight—who do we appreciate? Garbage!

A loud chorus of voices crowded in on Scrappy's imagination. She could not stand it. Somehow, they had to be silenced. But how? She would think of a way.

Practice was at five.

"Hi ya, Scrappy," said Hughie. "You finally decided."

"I'm here," she said.

"Hi, Scrappy."

"How you doin', Scrappy?"

Just about everyone seemed glad to see her.

"Oh, hello," said Mary Louise, coming on the field two minutes late. "How was the wedding?"

"It was okay. I'm a sister-in-law now."

"Congratulations. Are you coming out for the team?"

"If they want me."

"I imagine we can use you. But you won't be starting in Monday's game with Footwear," the coach informed her. "We have six extra players—seven now, counting you. No one is a substitute, in this club. Everyone plays. But a starting place in the lineup has to be earned."

"I guess I deserve that," thought Scrappy, who in more than one game for old Garage had been voted Most Valuable Player and now was wearing her old, faded Garage jersey.

"Come over to the shop sometime before Monday, and I'll issue you a uniform," said Mary Louise.

The coach now turned to the squad, who were doing the usual—taking shots on the goal with half a dozen balls going at once, the goalie going crazy trying to stop them. "All right, gang. Let's settle down and do a little work. Right now, I want you to split up and form three circles. We'll practice heading. Just see how long you can keep the ball in the air."

The squad divided into three groups of six each

and started bouncing balls from head to head, around and back and forth across the circle. To someone passing by on the Common, it might look strange, but plenty of goals are scored off a player's skull and plenty are saved that way, as well. It was a drill that Joe had never given the team, and it was one of the things that was paying off in the team's standing in the league, which now was in a tie for third with Perkins Nurseries. It was nice to look forward to playing on a winning team, and Scrappy now had no doubt who was responsible for the big improvement. Too bad the team had to lose the coach right now. Scrappy headed one toward Gregg, but it was too low, and all he could do was butt it into the ground. Mary Louise joined Scrappy's circle then and neatly headed every one that came to her, high and to where a player could get under it and keep it aloft. It was more than Joe could ever have tried to do. Joe was clompy. After that first flub, Scrappy did well, and on one rally her circle kept the ball up for nineteen bounces without a miss.

"Really great," Mary Louise said, then lined the squad up for passing practice. "The real secret of winning is good passing," she repeated. Even Scrappy had heard her say that before, at that first practice, when she was on the sidelines. But no one minded, because they had found out that it was true, and they were getting really sharp at it.

"The game with Hot Tubs, last week, was pitiful," Freddy Monkton told Scrappy. "We played rings around them—just kept possession. Shots! We took dozens of shots! We owned the ball."

"What was the score?"

"Two, nothing."

"How come only two, if we were so great?"

"Their goalie is pretty good."

"Good! He must be terrific. I wish I had been in that game." Scrappy was thinking of the shots she'd have booted past that Hot Tubs goalie.

They finished practice with fifteen minutes of scrimmage—crimson side of the jerseys against the gold—nine against nine. Scrappy, in her old Garage jersey, played midfield for the crimsons and played her best, which wasn't bad, considering she had not had a toe on a ball for over four weeks. It felt wonderful to be playing again. It felt nice, too, to have Mary Louise for a coach. Even in pants and a Mary Louise Shop jersey, the coach was pretty, Scrappy noticed. Pretty, but not the same as certain people Scrappy could mention.

"Way to go, Scrappy!" the coach called to the left halfback. Scrappy had just taken a very high ball on her cranium and headed it all the way across field to

Stu Patton, at right wing, causing her to see a shower of brightly colored stars. At that very instant, she had her great idea, and before practice was over, she had managed to spread the word throughout the squad. "After practice—a meeting over by the bicycle rack."

"Hey, what's up, Scrap?"

"You'll find out when you get there. Pass the word."

21

Practice was over, and soon the entire squad had drifted over to the meeting place, wondering what Scrappy was plotting.

"All right. Everyone here?" Scrappy began.

"What's up?"

"We're getting a new sponsor," Scrappy announced.

"How come?"

"Who?"

"Nobody knows yet. It could be Elite."

"Elite what?"

"What's that? What's Elite?"

"Don't you know?" said Scrappy.

"No. We don't. What is it?"

"Elite Garbage Collection, naturally. What did you suppose?"

"Garbage!"

"Right."

Total groans.

"Oh, no!"

"I'm not playing!"

"Garbage?"

"What's wrong with being a walking billboard for garbage?" Norris Collins asked innocently.

"How come we're going to get a new sponsor?"

"How come?"

"How do you know?" A dozen questions crowded in on Scrappy.

She took a deep breath. "Her store is going to close, because not enough people come in to buy things. My mother and father told me, last night."

For a moment, everyone was quiet.

Finally, Todd asked, "What can we do?"

"Yeah, what can we do?"

Everyone wanted to know how they could help. They really liked Mary Louise and the way she coached. They liked to win. Certain boys, Scrappy noticed, even acted a little silly around her, but it wasn't the fault of Mary Louise, she decided. Most of all, they knew what they would be called by every kid in school, if Scrappy was right about the new sponsor. What could they do?

"Quiet!"

"Quiet!"

"That's what I'm going to tell you. Here's the

plan. Here are the main things we have to do," Scrappy began. "First . . ."

Scrappy's strategy meeting by the bicycle rack was Tuesday, after practice. Now it was Monday of the next week, the day of the big contest with Clemson's Footwear, generally known throughout the league as Shoe Store—except by Chester B. Clemson, who insisted on everyone calling it by its official name, in his hearing. It was to be the day of Scrappy's first appearance with the crimson No Names. In just that one week of practice, she had earned a starting place at left half.

Right now, Shoe Store was first in the standings. No Name was third. Both had pulled ahead of Quality Cleaners in the past weeks. A win over Shoe Store by No Name might tie them for first, depending on the outcome of three games being played on other fields in the county. The starting whistle would blow at five o'clock. It now was four-thirty, and Scrappy was standing on the post office steps, suited up for the game, waiting for her mother. She was wearing a light jacket over her jersey.

At four-thirty-two and a half, Mrs. Bassett eased her car into one of the parallel parking places across the Common from the post office, and Scrappy hurried over to meet her.

"You're late," Scrappy said.

"By two and a half minutes," her mother said. "You should try to be this punctual, once in a while."

"Me?"

"Yes, you. Now what is all this about meeting you here a whole half hour before the game?"

Scrappy thought for a minute about how to begin, then began. "Mom, I saw something in the window, down at Mary Louise's. A very cute dress —blue with little flowers on it."

"Yes, Scrappy?" Could this be her daughter talking?

"May I have it, please, for the Thanksgiving party at Grandma's?"

"That's a long time off. That's not until next fall."

"I know. I just want to have it so I can try it on when I feel like it."

"Why, Laura Jean!" said Mrs. Bassett, unable to keep the surprise out of her voice.

"Rick said I looked cute in a dress, at the wedding."

"I see," said her mother. "Rick noticed, did he?"

"Yes," said Scrappy. "Let's go. We only have twenty-five minutes."

"That's not very long to pick out a dress," said her mother.

"I've already picked it out," Scrappy said. "The day I went in to get my uniform."

"Oh, I see. Well, I'm not promising a thing."

They crossed the Common kitty-corner, to The Mary Louise Shop, where petunias were blooming healthily in a window box. Entering, they found both Mary Louise and her assistant, Susan, busy with customers—both of them mothers of boys who were on the team. One was looking at pandas of different sizes, the other at little-girl blouses.

"Kevin and Pete both have little sisters," Scrappy explained to her mother.

"Be with you very shortly," Mary Louise said.

"That's all right, Coach," Scrappy said. Mary Louise was not wearing a dress and high heels but her jogging suit and Adidas. Scrappy explained to her mother, "She'll put on her team jersey just before she goes over to the field."

It was not long before Mary Louise's customer had decided on a medium-sized panda, had it gift wrapped and had paid for it, leaving Mary Louise free to take care of Scrappy and her mother.

"My goodness!" said Mary Louise. "They were the tenth customers today who were parents of team members. You are the eleventh. What a nice coincidence, don't you think?"

"I should say so," said Mrs. Bassett. A very innocent expression came over Scrappy's face, and she said nothing.

"Well!" said Mary Louise. "What can I do for you?"

"The dress—you know which one—can I try it on?" Scrappy asked.

"I imagine you can." She seemed to be holding back, just a little. Could she be sure Mrs. Bassett would approve? She said, "Your daughter has been doing a little window shopping, as it were."

"I understand," Mrs. Bassett said. "It's quite all right. She may try it on, if she likes."

Mary Louise took a dress from its place on a rack and brought it out. "It's really a very pretty dress," she said.

"I know it," said Scrappy. "A girl in school has one exactly like it."

"Oh, yes. Floramae. Is she in your class?"

"Yes," said Scrappy.

"Is that all right with you?" her mother asked.

"Is what all right?" asked Scrappy, a little puzzled.

"Having a dress exactly like someone else's."

"Uh-huh. Why not?"

"No reason. No reason at all," her mother said, exchanging private glances with Mary Louise. Did they really think that Scrappy did not notice?

Grown-ups were really slow—when they thought you didn't see or understand. Scrappy knew perfectly well that her mother would rather die than meet somebody at a party wearing exactly the same kind of dress as she had on. Well, that was her mother's problem.

Scrappy got into the dress and looked at herself in the tall mirror, turning this way and that, smoothing it down, then twirling around to make it flare way out. She expected a comment or at least another exchange of secret looks that meant *What a change in Scrappy!* But neither her mother nor Mary Louise said a word, and their looks remained frozen, except for the possible hint of a little smile on Mary Louise's lips.

"Can I have it?" Scrappy asked, at last tearing herself away from the mirror.

"If you really like it," said her mother.

She wanted to say that she loved it and that it made her look twice as pretty as Floramae Williams, even with her hair still held back in a rubber band, for the game. "I like it all right," she said.

"Oh, well, if you're not more enthusiastic than that—"

"I love it! I really love it! I really do! I think it's darling."

"Very well," said her mother. "So do I. We'll take

it," and she wrote out a check, while Mary Louise wrapped up the dress.

In the meantime, three more mothers of boys on the team came in. They were on their way to the game and hadn't time to buy anything just then. "We just wanted to look in and say hello," Paul Finley's mother explained.

"Just make yourself at home," said Mary Louise.

"What a pretty little shop," said Ray Dobbs's mother. "I just love the flower boxes at the window."

"We'll be back very soon," said Gregg Jenkins' mother.

Scrappy was listening and beaming like a little lighthouse, while her mother looked as if she had just discovered a plot to steal the flagpole from in front of the Bagley police station, at the other end of the Common. "*You* are a scamp and a rascal," she said to Scrappy.

"Me?" said Scrappy.

22

Across the Common, sitting on the bottom row of the bleachers, Bruce Reilly's mother was talking to Paul Zack's father, who had come home from work in the city early to see this game. "Who'd ever have thought it, Pete?" Mrs. Reilly was saying. "Good old bad-news Garage is now in third place. And coached by a gal."

"You have to hand it to her," Mr. Zack agreed. "Another few weeks with that kind of coaching and no injuries and who knows what could happen?"

The bleachers were nearly filled, and people were strung out along the sidelines on both sides of the field. It was almost as large a crowd as for any championship play-off. Some were parents, but there were others, including members of the Youth Soccer Council and coaches of other teams, scouting the game. Someone said that the man snapping pictures all over the place was from the *Independent Journal*, which proved to be true, as readers of the local press discovered the following day.

"Wouldn't you just love to see our guys wipe out Footwear?" Mrs. Reilly remarked to Mr. Zack. Just about everyone knew that Footwear's coach and sponsor, Chester B. Clemson, was dead set against women and girls getting mixed up in boys' sports. If No Name beat Footwear, Clemson would have to eat crow.

"I'd give a lot to see that," said Mr. Zack.

"What do they call our team now, by the way?" Mr. Zack wondered. "It's not Garage anymore. Not with old Joe Palmer sunning himself in the Islands."

"The Mary Louise Shop, I suppose, is the official name."

"It doesn't say so on the jerseys."

"Don't you know what happened?"

"No."

"I'll tell you sometime. Listen to over there, will you!"

It was seven minutes to five, and Shoe Store was gathered at the west end of the field, where Chester B. Clemson was giving them a gung ho, do-or-die pep talk, telling them in a ringing voice that they had to win this one for their honor and the shoe store. "All right, gang," he was saying. "Get out there and take those turkeys apart. And just remember one thing. No team with a girl on it and coached by a . . . a . . ." He could hardly bring himself to say the word. ". . . a woman . . . is going to humble Clemson's Footwear."

The pep talk ended, and the team knelt in a huddle and solemnly placed their hands, one atop the other, on a soccer ball and gave the ax yell, which the coach led.

> Give 'em the ax, the ax, the ax.
> Give 'em the ax, the ax, the ax.
> Give em the ax, yea-a-a-ay!
> Footwear! Footwear! Footwear!

At just that moment, Scrappy Bassett, happy owner of a pretty, new dress—now locked safely in the trunk of her mother's car—charged onto the field to join her team, at the east end, nearest the Common. It was now four minutes to five, which gave her just about three minutes lead over her coach, who was taking care of one last customer.

"Hi, Scrappy. Where you been?" Hughie shouted.

"Is the coach coming?" Donald wanted to know. "It's almost five."

"Where is she? Where's Mary Louise?"

"Relax," said Scrappy. "She'll be here on time. So let's get set."

As Scrappy slipped off her jacket, which had covered her jersey, and tossed it on the players' bench, the entire squad lined up on the penalty arc, all facing the east goal. That way, they would be facing Mary Louise, as she came on the field. Scrappy joined them, squeezing in between Gregg and Peter. A few boys wriggled and giggled a little, but they soon settled down and stood still as statues and kept straight faces, while the man with the camera buzzed around, clicking away like a Geiger counter in a uranium mine, shooting pictures of the team from every angle. At the same time, a woman with a notebook was wandering around asking questions and making notes.

"Shhhhh!"

"Shhhhhhh!"

"Here she comes!"

"All right!" Scrappy said, in a loud whisper. "Don't forget—on THREE!"

No one breathed.

The time was twenty-eight seconds before five o'clock. Mary Louise, looking at her watch, hurried onto the east end of the field, looked up and stopped short. There was her whole squad—all eighteen of them—lined up in a semicircle, all facing front and standing at attention.

"What's all this about?" she was starting to say.

"One . . ." breathed Scrappy. "Two . . . THREE!"

On the count of three, every member of the

squad, excepting Scrappy—who forgot—turned around, showing the backs of their jerseys to Mary Louise. Then, suddenly remembering, so did Scrappy.

"One more time," said Scrappy and counted again. This time, on THREE, it was . . .

> Yea-a-a-ay Mary Louise!
> Yea-a-a-ay Mary Louise!
> Yea-a-a-ay Mary Louise!

The yell could be heard for half a mile around.

The camera clicked and caught the expression on the coach's face. Astonishment! Real honest-to-goodness surprise and no pretending! And then, with another click—happiness. For there on the back of every last crimson jersey were the words THE MARY LOUISE SHOP Not all the letters had been sewn back on in their original positions. Not all looked as if the sewing had been done by the players' mothers. Some letters may even have been stuck on with glue. But they were there. Mary Louise saw them. The people in the bleachers and on the sidelines saw them. Footwear saw them. The I-J photographer saw them and took a picture of them. There simply was no longer any doubt about the name of the team scheduled to play Footwear that afternoon —or of just which business in town was the team's sponsor. It was THE MARY LOUISE SHOP.

Seeing at once exactly what had happened, the coach rushed up to the squad and gathered into her arms as many players as she could reach and hugged them to her, bumping a few heads together as she did so. She was very strong. "You darlings!" she exclaimed. "All of you! You are the most adorable soccer team in the whole world and I love you dearly!"

Taken by surprise from behind, the boys who were getting hugged looked startled and embarrassed. But the others, including Scrappy, looked as if they had been left out of something and wanted to be included. Crowding closer to the center, most got their wish, as Mary Louise laughed and almost cried, both at the same time. It was quite strange.

Very shortly, after a few more pictures, including one of the two coaches shaking hands, the starting whistle blew and the game began. It was a hard-fought contest, and The Mary Louise Shop played a tremendous game, scoring two goals against first-place Footwear. But it wasn't quite good enough. Footwear scored three times, the final goal coming in the last two minutes of the game. Footwear had won, but it wasn't enough to save Chester B. Clemson from having to eat crow, especially since a girl had scored one of the goals against his best defense. Mary Louise had come very close to humbling Footwear, and almost no one who saw that game doubted for a minute that some day her team would do exactly that *if*—and it was a great big *if*—The Mary Louise Shop stayed open and in business and no other sponsor—Elite Garbage, for example—and a different coach took over in the weeks ahead. It was something nearly everyone in Bagley knew might happen, if business did not soon pick up for the shop on the Common. But, for right now, everyone in the bleachers and along the sidelines was very happy with the way things had worked out that afternoon—except, of course, certain Footwear parents, and even some of *them* were secretly delighted to see Chester B. Clemson served up a dish of tough, ill-tasting bird.

23

The one thing the Bassett family did without fail on Saturday mornings was sit down and have breakfast together. There was a special attraction, of course—buckwheat cakes with a choice of homemade raspberry-gooseberry topping or maple syrup. The buckwheat cakes were made right at the table, on a special grill, and they were always delicious.

This Saturday morning, three weeks or so after the big game with Footwear, Mr. Bassett was stealing glances at the morning newspaper, between bites. Reading at Saturday morning breakfast was not permitted—his own rule—but he was being cautious.

"We had a letter yesterday from Mike and Pam," Mrs. Bassett announced.

"Are they making ends meet?" asked Scrappy.

"What!" said Josh. He was forever being astonished at senseless questions his sister asked. Senseless to him, at least.

"I'll read you the whole letter, when we finish breakfast," her mother said. Mr. Bassett had gotten in late, the night before, from an out-of-town trip, and she had been saving it.

"I was reading your Kung Fu book," Josh said.

"Oh, that," said Scrappy.

"I'll fight you just as soon as I finish reading it."

"You blew your chance. I'm a soccer player now."

"You mean you won't fight me? Aw, heck, I've read half the book already."

"I'll sell it to you for fifty cents," Scrappy offered.

"With no one to fight, what good will the book do me?"

"Give me fifty cents, then, and I'll fight you."

"You're on," said Josh. "I owe you fifty cents. This afternoon?"

"Not this afternoon. We're scouting a game—me and Hughie."

"What team are you scouting?"

"Ice Cream Parlor. We're tied with them for first. We want to watch their tactics from the sidelines."

"Isn't that a new one?" asked Mrs. Bassett.

"Just a new name," Scrappy explained. "They used to be Car Wash."

"What ever happened to Shoe Store?" Josh wondered.

"We sunk them the second time we played them —four to one. They never came back up again. They're down to fourth."

"Chet Clemson has sure come down off his high horse," said Mr. Bassett. He was talking about Shoe Store's sponsor and coach. "A girl scoring against his team twice was more than he could handle."

"Nice going, Scrap," said Josh, and Scrappy made her Bugs Bunny face.

"You must learn to say, 'Thank you,' when somebody compliments you," said Mrs. Bassett.

"Thanks," said Scrappy.

Mr. Bassett, who had given up pretending not to be reading the paper, said, "No doubt about it, The Mary Louise Shop is making it big. Look at this." He opened the paper wide to where he was reading. "A whole quarter page. Now, that's an expensive ad for a small business."

"Oh, she's making money," Mrs. Bassett agreed. "No doubt about it. I never go past but what her shop appears to be full of people."

"That's what comes of sponsoring a winning soccer team," Josh said. "Take a bow, Scrap."

Scrappy crammed a double forkful of wheatcakes into her mouth.

"She's going to be a very busy lady," said Mrs. Bassett.

"Not too busy to coach," said Scrappy, when she could talk.

Mr. Bassett studied his daughter, as she worked on her stack, lubricating it well with raspberry-gooseberry topping and maple syrup. Was this a good time to say the thing he was thinking seriously of saying? Well, it had to be said, sooner or later. "Scrappy?"

Scrappy looked at her father and nodded.

"When is your next soccer practice?"

She swallowed, finally, and said, "Monday. Why?"

Mr. Bassett still was not sure—was it better to let Scrappy find out on Monday, or prepare her for it now? "Listen," he said, finally. "Monday, at practice, you may get some interesting news."

Scrappy looked alert, like a watchful rabbit.

"Mary Louise is giving up the team," her father informed her.

"What?" Scrappy exclaimed.

"One of the busiest times of day for Mary Louise is late afternoon," her mother explained. "She simply has to be there to take care of customers."

"You've got to be kidding," said Scrappy. "How do you know?"

"Word gets around, downtown," Mr. Bassett said. He belonged to the Chamber of Commerce and the Rotary Club.

"The skunk!" exclaimed Scrappy. "We never should have put her name back on our jerseys. We shouldn't have told people to go into her store and buy stuff. That's what did it. My great idea!"

"If you hadn't, she probably would have gone out of business and had to let the team go, anyway," her father reasoned.

"I hate her," said Scrappy.

"I don't think you mean that," said her mother.

"Yes, I do. Not only that. She's ungrateful. Also disloyal. After all we did for her. Oh, wow! This is gross."

"Come off it, Scrap," said her brother. "You only saved her so you wouldn't be called Garbage. Admit it."

"I won't admit it!"

"Oh, you wanted to be called Garbage?"

"Stop confusing me. Daddy, make Josh stop confusing me. Sure, we would rather be called Mary Louise than . . . than . . ." She could not bring herself to say it. "Now that we're first, it doesn't matter if they call us Mary Louise. And if you want to know, we really like our coach. She's really neat." Miserably, Scrappy added, "At least I thought so—until she did this to us."

"Looks as if you're in a no-win situation," her father said.

"We're in first place," Scrappy objected. "What do you mean?"

"It's just an expression, dear," her mother explained. "What your father is saying is that whether Mary Louise stayed in business or failed, you'd have to lose her—and Elite would be your sponsor, after all."

"That's for positively certain?" Scrappy asked.

"Certain," said her father.

"Then you knew, all along. Why didn't you tell me?"

"I'm telling you now. I just heard it yesterday at lunch."

"What did you hear, exactly?" Scrappy demanded.

"That it's all set. Elite's going to be your new sponsor. And I doubt very much that Jim Campbell's going to let you get away with ripping the sponsor's name off your jerseys. Not if I know Jim."

"This is the end," said Scrappy. "The living end."

"My sister plays left halfback for Elite Garbage," said Josh, rolling the words deliciously on his tongue.

"Don't be mean to your sister," said Mrs. Bassett.

"Josh Bassett's sister plays halfback for Garbage," her brother persisted. "I don't think I'd want that noised around town. I have my reputation to think about. I just don't know."

Scrappy slipped out of her chair, careened around the table and started for Josh, her arm cocked for a karate chop to the jugular. Josh put up both elbows and took the blow on his right forearm.

"Ouch!" cried Scrappy, shaking her hand in pain. "Your bones are sharp."

"Kids!" their father commanded. "Knock it off! Scrappy! Back to your place! Sit down!"

Grimly, Scrappy returned to her place at the table. "The whole team will simply quit," she announced.

"At the top of the league, I wouldn't care what they called me," her father said.

"Top of the league! Without our coach, the team is a dead duck," Scrappy declared. She was very downhearted.

"Why not give your new coach a chance?"

"Why bother?"

"I have news for you."

"I've heard enough news."

"You don't know a single thing about Jim Campbell."

"No, and I don't care to. He's some guy who collects garbage."

"What about the lady who sold pretty dresses?" her mother reminded her.

"That was different," Scrappy countered. "Nobody knew that she was a great player, in her day.

And a skunk," she added, under her breath.

"Who knows what your new coach might have been, in *his* day?" her father asked, as if he knew something she didn't know.

Scrappy shrugged.

"Do you really think you might resign again?" asked Josh. "How many times would that be—five? Or six?"

"I don't want to talk about it," Scrappy said, beginning to slide out of her chair. "Excuse me, please."

"Finish your breakfast first," said her mother.

Scrappy stuffed down the remnants of her second stack, drained her glass, left the table and trudged off to her room.

Monday afternoon—time for practice. Scrappy was suited up, wearing her new cleats, which had been approved by the Council just the previous week. But she was still sitting on her bicycle, the front wheel lodged in the rack, looking past the bleachers at those players who had arrived early and already were milling about by the east goal, practicing high corner kicks and headers. Scrappy herself had very little heart for going out on the field. After all that she and the others had done to save The Mary Louise Shop and their coach—even climbing right to the top of the ratings—it now seemed certain, from what her father had said, that Mary Louise was about to let them down. This meant a take-over of the team by some new guy who would probably stamp the garbage name on the back of their jerseys in some way that no one could remove it. This would really shake the team up, blow their minds, and probably cause a mass revolt and mass resignations. The new guy didn't know what he had to deal with, in taking over. Scrappy was determined to play, if anyone did, no matter what, but right now she wasn't charging out on the field, all gung ho and steaming to get into the action.

Then she saw Mary Louise come across the Common, from her store, and walk over to the east goal. Scrappy's spirits bounded into outer space. What if Mary Louise had changed her mind and decided to stay on as coach, after all? Locking up her bike, she was off like a shot and pulled up to a saunter only as she rounded the bleachers and came on the field.

"Hi, Scrap," said Pete Johnson, the right fullback.

"Hi," said Scrappy. "What's new?"

"Nothing," said Pete. Obviously the word had not gotten out yet—if it was true. Scrappy hoped that it wasn't, that her father somehow or other had heard it all wrong. She started across the field, where Mary Louise, Doug Preston, and Bruce

Reilly, forming a small triangle, were casually passing a ball among themselves with short side-foot taps. Nothing unusual about that. Not half the squad was on the field yet—it was still a little early —or Mary Louise would have had them organized in some general drill, like the whole team moving up and down the field a few times, dribbling and passing left to right and then back again, as they went. Nothing unusual except that Mary Louise herself was early and seemed to be stalling along, waiting for something. Joining the triangle, making it a square now, Scrappy could hardly resist asking if what she had heard was true or, if it was, had Mary Louise changed her mind and decided to stay on as coach? If only she would. Scrappy really liked Mary Louise—loved her, she would almost have said, even if some of the boys acted silly about her. It wasn't her fault—she was nice, but all the same, skunko, if she let them down.

A few minutes passed and it was time now to begin real practice. Nearly the whole team was on the field. All except Hughie Digby, who had to have his cavities checked that afternoon, and Scrappy knew he was going to miss practice. The team had become very prompt, and attendance was almost perfect, since Mary Louise had taken over—but right now nothing was happening. Then a car was

seen scooting into a parking place on the Common
—a small dark green Triumph, with its top down.
Mary Louise took special notice of it, turning away
from Scrappy and the two boys in the square. A
man got out of the car, slammed the door with a
muffled thud, came through the gap in the hedge
that separated the Common from the soccer field
and walked briskly toward the east goal. He looked
about as old as Scrappy's father, though not quite as
tall and very much stockier. He had graying short
curly hair and a long face and a long, humorous
nose. He wore slacks and a sports jacket over a dark
red tennis shirt. He walked over to where Mary
Louise stood and, as they shook hands and exchanged greetings, everything became crystal clear
to Scrappy. This man did not look like her idea of
a garbage collector. No doubt he merely owned the
company and didn't do any of the work. But he had
to be the new coach, and Mary Louise was here
today just to introduce him to the team and say
good-bye. It was Skunk City, after all. This was it.

Scrappy was right.

"Team," Mary Louise began. All had gathered
around—something was happening. "As you surely
know, coaching you has been one of the really wonderful experiences of my life. I've loved it, and I love
all of you. But now, as things have turned out—due

very largely to your own efforts—my little store is doing so well that I simply can't spare the time to go on coaching. And so now I want you to meet my replacement, your new sponsor, who I'm sure you will find to be the best coach you have ever had. Jim Campbell, meet your team."

The man smiled a humorous, cracked smile, as if someone had just made a joke about him, gave a little nod to Mary Louise, and said, "I'm sure I've got a tough act to follow, Ma'am. I've heard nothing but the best about your coaching and your leadership. And of course your team is right up there in the ratings."

Wow! He even talked funny.

"He's Scotch!" whispered Doug Preston to Scrappy. "He talks just like my grandmother, who came over here from Scotland."

"Scotch?"

Mary Louise continued. "Jim owns his company, but it has been here a long time, and he has promised me that, no matter how good business becomes, he will always have time to coach a soccer team. Jim's company, by the way, is called Elite, and *that*," she said, with a wry smile, "is all that will ever be on the backs of your jerseys."

"Garbage . . . !"

"Garbage . . . !"

"Garbage . . . !"

The word moved like wildfire, in whispers, through the team. ELITE it might be on the jerseys, but they knew what it would be in the mouths of every last kid in the town of Bagley. This was the pits.

"Now, in turning you over to Jim, I have to tell you something I know he would be too modest to tell you, himself."

Mr. Campbell looked embarrassed and said, "I wish you wouldn't, Ma'am."

"No, this is essential and very appropriate," Mary Louise insisted. "Mr. Campbell is a Scot—from Scotland—as perhaps you can tell from his name and from his nice way of talking."

"Just like my grandmother," Doug repeated. "It's called a burr."

"Scotland, as perhaps you know, is where the game was invented."

"What game?" whispered Stu Patton.

"Scrabble, stupid!" That was J. P. Hudson, always clowning.

"Scotland has always fielded a strong team in World Cup competition," Mary Louise went on.

Scrappy was getting some kind of strong signals from Mary Louise's voice, and they were good signals, although she could not quite read them.

"Jim played for Scotland—center half—in the—"

"Please don't tell them what year," he interrupted. "It was some time ago."

"All right," said Mary Louise. "But it doesn't matter. I think you all get the message."

The silence out there in front of the east goal was thunderous. Nobody spoke. There was nothing but deep awe and silence among the players. They scarcely breathed. A player on a national World Cup team was going to coach them, at every practice. It was as if Pete Rose or maybe Reggie Jackson, after he retired, was going to be the regular coach of some Little League ball club in Bagley. No one could talk. There was nothing they could think of to say. That man, standing right there in front of them, had played in the World Cup, maybe even against Pelé, himself. Oh, wow! Scrappy could hardly keep herself from asking him if he had. Some day, at practice, she would, she was very sure.

"Well, then," said Mary Louise, breaking the spell. "I've got to get back to the store. Good luck, Jim. I know you'll get on fine with these great kids."

It was then that all pandemonium broke loose. Yells and hoots and hollers of every kind rent the silence. The one that a person coming out of the post office, across the Common, would have noticed most and thought a little strange sounded something like "Yea-a-a-ay! Ha-a-a-ay! We're going to be Numero Uno! Yea-a-a-ay! Numero Uno! Call us Garbage! Call us Garbage! Yea-a-a-a-ay!" And before long, the whole squad had taken up the cry—*Call us Garbage!*

Only Scrappy was quiet, trying to reach Mary Louise before she crossed the Common, to her store. She didn't say anything, just came up close beside Mary Louise, wanting to put an arm around her waist. But Mary Louise thought of it first and hugged Scrappy's shoulders, as they walked along. Neither had a single word to say.

At the curb, they stopped and separated, and Scrappy said, "I'll be seeing you around."

"I hope so," said Mary Louise. "After all, we're just across the Common."

She waved good-bye and crossed the Common to her store, and Scrappy went back to the field. She could hardly wait until after practice, when she could speed home and telephone Hughie Digby. She could hardly wait to hear him react to the news. It would blow his mind.